I0529705

The Tree
at
Lindley Park

Annette Stephenson

Acknowledgements

To my loving husband for giving me courage, strength, and most of all love. You are inspiring and bring light into my life each day. Thank you for your beautiful art pieces and everything I've learned from you. I love you

Giving love to my children and grandchildren.

From childhood on, I have been writing my emotions and thoughts to give others my gift of storytelling. Thank you to all those who love my books and give support. Playing my piano gives a calm to my thoughts and soothes my soul.

Copyright 2021

Prologue

Cara Sanderson came into this world not knowing her parents. No family came forward to adopt her as an infant. She had seen her share of foster homes during her tender years. Some homes had love, good memories, and friends she would be forced to say goodbye to. Other homes were less welcoming. When she felt alone and missed her previous foster family, she would sit in her closet and draw; art pieces inspired where she could travel to and maybe live in when she grew up. These thoughts were kept for herself, fearing someone taking away her hope for a better life.

Her heart constantly searched. She looked for places to find peace during restless thoughts. After school, she loved the sweet release of walking by nice landscapes, wooded areas, and the park. Even though it was the long way, she would look forward to the time of day when she could just be where she felt happy. Watching the seasons change the leaves made her warm and comfortable. Children played, mothers walked their babies, or someone walked their dog. Cara's gaze eventually settled at the center where there grew a very old and large tree. Several children were climbing on its branches. She noticed odd textures on its bark. As she neared it, she realized it was full of carvings. There were initials, hearts, and names. Some of the children climbed to the very top of the tree, not paying any mind to the artwork of the carvers. Since Cara taught herself how to draw, she planned to sketch this tree, bringing out all its beauty. To her, it made her happy because it was full of history. She longed to be part of that. Little did she know, someone was observing. He smiled a little each time he saw her.

At home she would look in the mirror and wonder who she looked like. She wanted to believe that she had features just like her mother. Somedays it was easy to envision it was her mother smiling back and talking to her. Her imagination was filled with pleasant conversations and warm attention. Was her mother talented and vibrant? She often wondered why she was given away. There was no answer to that perplexing question or any reason to place pointless stress on the thought. Cara would create stories about her mother, imagining her as an artist or a ballet dancer. It made her feel like her own story was not about abandonment but something greater, beautiful and wistful.

As a young girl, Cara would sit beneath the tree to gather inspiration. She would put all thought and emotion into her artistic expressions. Afterward, adding a heartfelt poem would bring it to life. After many visits to the park, Cara decided to put her mark on the tree. Up as high as she could go, she would carve her own initials.

Now a grown young woman nearing thirty, Cara has memories of the tree at Lindley Park. Life improved because it and shaped much of her future. How did a tree influence a woman's destiny? What created such a change for the better? She recalls a time years ago in San Diego, the place where Cara Jo Sanderson came into the world.

Chapter 1

The Quiet Goodbye

A woman lived alone in a small home with her baby. She was wrapping her to go out. Looking at the face of her beautiful daughter, tears began to fall thinking about the decision she had to make. A mother who gave birth to her first child should be happy. In this case, a mother is scared and alone without her mate to share those memories with. There was no other choice at the time. She had to protect her daughter and hope she would have a good life. She was wrapped warm and fed as she put her in her car seat to be safe. The woman reached her destination and proceeded to get out of the car. She talked to her child, whispering how much she loved her. She stared into her eyes for a few minutes. She knew in her mind she couldn't go back on her decision, and it was breaking her heart.

The late evening was always quiet in the hospital. The waiting room and visiting lounge had seated only three people. No one noticed a young woman who quietly arrived with a sleeping baby wrapped in her arms. She didn't know who to talk to about her situation. A nurse observed and felt compelled to approach her tenderly.

"Excuse me, Miss. Can I help you?" she asked.

"No, thank you. May I sit here?"

"You have a beautiful baby. Is she needing medical assistance?"

The woman didn't answer and continued looking at the floor. She couldn't help but notice that this woman looked very young and appeared to be afraid. Sympathetically, she sat next to her.

"Miss, are you sure you're, okay?"

The young woman tried to hold her emotions together, but she was overcome with tears. She slowly looked up and asked, "Would you like to hold her?"

"Sure. I have a baby of my own. How old is she?"

"She was born 2 months ago."

"What's your baby's name?"

"Cara Jo Sanderson."

"That's a pretty name."

Nervously, she started looking around. Her hands were trembling.

"Miss, I am a good listener. If you feel the need to talk, you can trust me."

"I'll be fine. I just want to sit here for a moment."

"Can you tell me your name?"

The woman didn't want to answer any questions. She didn't want to purge her feelings to this kind nurse.

"I want my daughter to have a good life. She deserves better."

"I'm sure you can give her a very good life."

"I'm so young and alone. I just want her to be happy."

The nurse adjusted herself to give the baby back. The mother touched her daughter's hair and stood up. She quickly turned and hurried away as the nurse called out, "Miss, wait! Come back! Miss!"

No one was able to find the mother again or discover why she abandoned her child. Baby Cara was now without a family. Her mother didn't want to leave her with just anyone. She trusted the hospital would find a good home for her. The staff was saddened to see a baby left to be cared for by someone else, by strangers. The hospital called Child Protective Services to find her a foster home. The nurse never forgot the woman's eyes filled with fright and insecurity. She appeared clean and healthy and a decent person. What was her reason? Something went very wrong in her life. What had happened? As Cara's mother ran out of the hospital, she disappeared into the night. She opened the door to an empty home sobbing. With little strength, she fell upon her bed scared by what she had done. She cried out in loud sounds of weeping as she held a picture that is the only memory she can look upon. She wants what she lost to come back and in reality; it will never be the same again. What did she lose? She had no money, no life left in her to think clearly. Distraught by her actions, she would need help to start her life over again. It was time for her to sleep. The next day she would gather the strength and courage to move on. She didn't change her clothes as she fell asleep crying. Laying on her bed, she had no covers over her body. She was curled in a ball holding tight to the photograph. Her story would be tucked away for now. She needed to start again. Will she ever lead a normal life after her loss?

Chapter 2

I Will Never Forget You

Cara was placed with a family who had a nice home where there were other children. Unfortunately, they could only care for her a short while. Each placement was a temporary one for this beautiful brunette who would steal anyone's heart with her adorable smile. By the age of eight, Cara was placed with the Grier family. Her favorite place was Lindley Park, a place where her foster mother took her and the other fostered children to play. It was a few blocks around the corner from her school, and as Cara grew up, she would walk by the park, sitting on one of the benches to look at the trees. At age fourteen, she noticed one of the larger trees farther back had children climbing to the top, something she hadn't paid attention to before. Cara never climbed a tree and she was curious as to why the kids were attracted to its branches. It was time for Cara to stop being an observer and take a chance to find out more.

Getting closer, she noticed some of the children carving their names on its bark. She thought how beautiful it was to see so many markings from different people. Some even wrote small messages and thoughts with the year next to the initials. She climbed up, trying her best to pull herself up to the top. Her attempt was not successful. A young boy noticed Cara and called out to her. He had seen her before, but only at a distance. He put out his hand to help her up.

"Hey, do you want to put your name on it?" he asked.

"Are you talking to me?"

"Yeah. Do you want to carve something?"

"Sure, but I don't have anything to carve with."

"Here, you can use my pocketknife. It's special. My grandma gave it to me last year." He climbed down towards her.

"Come on. Climb up here."

Cara didn't know how to use a pocketknife. The young boy wanted her to come up and sit with him. He helped her climb up to get a better look.

"Do you need help using it?" he asked.

"Can you show me?"

The young boy started to carve a star on the bark.

"Watch me, then try it. Do you think you can do it now?"

"Yes."

She slowly began to carve something, feeling a bit inadequate.

"Am I doing it right?"

"Yep. There's no wrong way to do it. Write anything you want. Just don't cut yourself."

"Where is your name?" Cara asked.

"Mine is way up there. I'm T.J."

"I'm Cara. Do you come here often?"

"Yeah, after school."

"I love to come here. I've always loved this tree, but I never looked at it close enough to see those names."

"Everybody puts their name on the tree. Some even put love hearts, you know stuff like that."

"It's like reading a book.

"What do you mean?"

9

"Well, it's all different, different names and styles of writing. It's artistic."

"You talk like an adult."

"I like art. I can draw, you know."

"Really? I don't have any talents."

"I'm sure you have at least one."

No, not one. My friends all take music lessons or sports but not me. I don't mind. What do you draw?"

"Oh, animals like horses and birds. I really like trees."

"You should show me your drawings sometime."

"I'd like that. Does your mom let you come here a lot?" Cara asked.

"My mom knows I'm here, but I can't stay too long. I live around the corner," T.J. replied.

"I live close too."

T.J. looked at Cara's initials.

"C.S. Do you want to write anything else?"

"Do I have to?"

"No. Maybe on another day you can think of something else to say."

"What does T.J. stand for?"

"Thomas James. That was my dad's name. My name is Bryan Dawson. My mom started calling me T.J. because I looked like my dad."

"He must be proud you took on his name."

"No, he died when I was five. I've seen pictures of him. My mom said he was a good guy."

"I'm sorry. I never knew my mother."

"Do you live with your dad?"

"No, I live in a foster home. It's not like a real family. There so many rules and when I make a friend, they get adopted or they move to a different home."

"I have a stepdad. He's not what you would call my favorite dad of the year. I understand what you mean about having a real family."

Cara handed the pocketknife back to T.J.

"I wish I could stay longer. I should go home. I've stayed later than I should have."

"Will you come back?" T.J. asked.

"Yes. I promise."

"Does your foster mom mind if you stay longer next time you come?"

"I would have to ask her. I'm glad I met you, T.J."

"Bye, Cara."

After climbing down, she looked back up at her new friend still in the branches. He was still watching.

She wanted to return desperately. There was something about this boy that made her feel as if she were home. Cara wanted a real family. In her mind, T.J. could be her family.

The next day, she raced with anticipation as she spotted him.

"Hey, I'm back."

"Come on up," waved T.J. She was cautious as she climbed slowly.

She had a new perspective about the tree that day. She had something to look forward to. She made a friend, and she knew she bonded with him in a special way. It wasn't like a boyfriend, but someone she could relate to.

"What's new today? Should we write something in a different spot?" Cara asked.

"I don't know what we'd write."

"I think I would like to read some of the carvings," Cara said feeling interested.

"I'm not much into reading."

"What do you do when you are alone, I mean, what activities are you in to?"

"I'm not sure I should tell you what I do when I'm alone."

She noticed his voice changed to sad.

"I'm your friend. You can tell me anything. What is it?"

T.J. had a reason he loved to be in the tree at the park. It was a place to escape an environment he wasn't happy in. Living in a home where a child felt safe wasn't the home T.J. lived in. He missed his natural father and thought about how things changed after his mother married Jackson Perry.

"I come here to get away. There is no fear up here, even if I climb up high, I feel free without being afraid of anything."

"What do you have to be afraid of?" Cara quizzed.

He lowered his voice. "My home is not the happiest place for a kid. My stepdad fights with my mom all the time. One time, he threw a glass at the wall, and it scared me."

"Oh, I'm sorry. Have you talked to anyone about this?"

"No. I don't want to start trouble or get him mad at me. Besides, I'm getting used to hearing it."

"No one should ever get used to hearing arguments or being yelled at. Has he ever hit you?"

"Um, he just yells. He has a vicious temper. He leaves for days, and things get better. But then it starts again when he comes back. I hear my mother cry at night."

"T.J., I wish I could help."

"I just can't wait to grow up and leave. My mother wishes things would get better, but if he were not here to support us, that would make things harder for Mom and I."

"Do you have any brothers or sisters?"

"No. I always wished I had a brother to confide in. Someday I want to do something for my mom. She deserves a better life and I'm going to make that happen."

He grew tired talking about the stresses in his home life. He wanted to find out more about Cara.

"So, what's your story? How did you end up in foster homes?"

"I really don't know the whole story. A counselor told me my mother gave me away at a hospital. I never had any family, so I just went to foster care. My wish is to get adopted someday, but families only want babies."

"Do you like where you live now?"

"I do. Marcia is nice. She is the one person who seems like a real mom, more than the other caretakers. She looks out for me. She can be strict sometimes."

"I think about what it would be like if I went away."

"Oh, don't say that. Have you ever thought that your mother needs you? I'm sure she's happy she has you in her life." Cara was concerned about how T.J. felt at that moment.

"We used to have a few good times when she first got married. I'm not sure what went wrong and maybe I don't want to know."

"Thank you for telling me your story," she said quietly.

"Why?"

"I feel like we can support each other and that's what makes a strong friendship."

"I'm glad I met you. I think we will always be friends."

"Remember when you said that you wished you had a brother to tell your troubles to? You can have me as your family. Don't you think there is something special between us?"

"I've never told anyone about my story before. You are so understanding without judging me. I used to see you at the park over there. You were sitting on that bench, and I wanted to ask why you are sitting alone."

"I've never climbed a tree until I met you. You helped me be brave enough to conquer my fear."

She smiled knowing she had something special with T.J.

"Oh no, what time is it?" she said anxiously.

"What's wrong?"

"I'm late. I gotta go."

"Will I see you again soon?"

"I'll be back."

"Don't say it if you don't mean it." He didn't want her to leave.

"I'll see you tomorrow."

He waved back knowing this was the best conversation he had with anyone he just met. The anxiety crept in thinking about going home to a place that felt like a living nightmare. T.J. felt hesitant to leave his perch.

He walked into his small home. He thought about helping his mom fold the laundry and then finish his homework. This gave him an hour of quiet before his parents came home. It was the only time this home felt calm.

Rushing to get home, Cara ran into the Grier house to find her foster mom waiting by the door.

"Cara, where have you been?"

"I went to the park. I didn't mean to be late."

"I gave you permission to go to the park, but you are late, and you had me worried."

"I know. I met a friend, we got to talking and..."

"Well, there is a penalty for being late. Now you are to come straight home from school and no visits to the park. You also have an early bedtime tonight. Go wash up to help prepare dinner."

"I won't be late again. Please give me another chance," Cara pleaded.

She realized that she made a promise to T.J. to be there. She suddenly felt sad that she would have to break it.

"I'm sorry. The answer is no. When you break a rule, you have to learn."

Cara was sad but she knew Marcia had a job to do. She was responsible for her safety and well-being. After doing the dishes, she went to her room to finish her homework. Sitting at her desk, she thought about T.J. and how she felt an attachment to him. The issues he was having at home were disturbing. He needed her support. What was he going to feel like when he discovered she wasn't there? She was going to have to wait out what may be a storm in the life of her good friend. She had to put her thoughts to rest.

This home was the warm haven she enjoyed, not like some of the others. The other homes weren't bad, she just didn't feel like she belonged. Being alone, she would have those times when she would cry missing a real mother. This was the longest Cara had ever stayed in a home. She had been living with the Grier family for five years. All those years she had been to that same park observing all its beauty and wished she could put it all on paper. The best part of her school library were the many books on art. She found one that taught pencil drawing. Her teacher gave her a sketch pad and some color pencils to practice with. Every day she would teach herself to draw different things. Nature was her luxury of human enjoyment. It was her way of getting rid of everything that made her sad.

The next day, T.J. looked for Cara. He was disappointed when she did not show up. He found her initials and above her name, he inscribed his real name, B.D. He waited as long as he could, but she never appeared. He could feel tears trying to fall. Her presence was a release of the pain living inside a dysfunctional family.

Several days later, Cara was able to go to the park again. She looked around for T. J. hoping she could talk to him again. Near the top of the tree, she spotted him sitting alone. She called out, but he didn't respond.

"T.J.! It's me, Cara!"

He didn't say a word to her.

"Come down, I want to talk to you," she called out.

He appeared frozen in his spot, so Cara did what she had to do to speak to him. She proceeded to climb.

"What's wrong? Why won't you answer me?"

Quietly he asked, "Where were you? I waited for you to come, and you never showed up."

"I broke a rule and couldn't leave the house. I really wanted to be here."

"I know this is going to sound stupid, but I hate promises that get broken."

"Why should that sound stupid?"

"Every day I sat up here waiting for you. It makes me happy to have you here. Do you understand what that means?" He was quiet with his head bowed, almost whispering his emotions.

"I do. I thought about you those days I sat in my room wishing I could be here. I know you needed me because I really needed you."

He looked at her with a small smile even though it was forced.

"Well, since you said that, I should forgive you. I guess it doesn't matter now."

"Why?"

"My parents are moving. This is my last day."

"Where are you going?"

"San Francisco. Jackson got a new job."

"I can't believe it. I'll never see you again."

"I wanted to see you that day we were supposed to meet to give you the news. I don't want to go."

"It's going to be weird without you. Each time I am here it won't be the same. I don't want you to go."

She paused trying not to feel lost in the announcement that she may have to live her life without him nearby. Then she found an idea.

"Let's write something. When I come by, I'll read it and remember when we had our last time at the tree."

She found it difficult to say. Cara was very upset inside that he was leaving.

"What should we write?"

"Well, the date is important. I like to write poems."

"Isn't that girly?" he smirked.

"No. There are many writers, men and women that penned beautiful poems. It's like writing a song. Let's see, how should it go?"

Cara tried hard to think of what this day meant to her and T.J. Anyone she became friends with would leave or be left behind. That was always difficult. She saw it happen many times. Cara always expected to be adopted and uprooted from her present world. She wanted to embrace their last moment without feeling that same void. She wasn't losing a friend; she gained a meaningful and close friendship. She may have not had much time to get to know him, but she was grateful they connected.

"I got it. It doesn't have to be long. Just enough to have a special meaning."

"You think this is special? Cara, can I say something to you?"

"Sure. What is it?"

"I think you're special."

She looked into his eyes, "I feel the same way about you."

She started to write from her heart.

There is a tender moment

When you meet someone special.

Today marks the day our friendship stayed

Even though you must go away. I will never forget you,
T.J.   Cara

She wrote this on a piece of paper and handed it to him. He carved the date and the words, *Friendship Forever T.J. and Cara.*

What they had was stronger than anything Cara expected. T.J. smiled holding on to the note she wrote. They were fourteen and what they meant to each other on their last day was priceless. They stayed in the tree for what seemed like hours. T.J. reached over to hold Cara's hand treasuring every minute that went by. When the time came to say goodbye, it was heartbreaking for the two of them. They couldn't help but hug each other hoping to never lose touch. They both agreed to write as much as they could. Cara was moved to tears fearing she would lose touch indefinitely.

T.J. came home to see boxes packed in the living room and kitchen and his room empty except for the mattress on the floor. His mother was in the kitchen cleaning.

"T.J. is that you?" she asked.

"Yeah, Mom. When are we leaving?"

"Tomorrow morning, the movers are coming early."

"Where's Jackson?"

"He's in the garage."

T.J. wanted to talk to him briefly. He was headed to the garage when his mother stopped him.

"Honey, it's not a good time right now."

"It's never a good time with him."

"Now, just give him some space. You are going to like San Francisco. What do you think?"

"I don't know yet.

"I'm sure you'll adjust."

"Will you adjust? Are you finally going to be happy?" T.J. questioned.

"What do you mean?"

"Mom, you know what I mean. Jackson is not a good man. Do you get tired of him always being angry?'

"Yes, I do, but he provides for us, and you know he tries."

"I miss Dad. Don't you miss him?"

"Of course, I do. This is all we have right now. Try to make the best of it." Ella's voice was quiet but firm with her expression. "This move is what Jackson needs to settle down. We can see how it goes."

"I hope you're right. I'm going to take care of you someday, Mom."

"Oh, T.J., you are more than any mom could want. I know living with Jackson is hard for you. But I am so glad to have you."

"My friend Cara said that you need me. Is that true?"

"It is."

She looked deep into his brown eyes and rubbed his curly hair.

"I can't believe how much you look like your father. He had the same color eyes." She was feeling melancholy and held her son.

At that moment, Jackson came into the kitchen.

"What's wrong?" he asked sounding uncaring.

"Nothing's wrong. I just wanted to hug my son."

"He looks like something's wrong." Jackson was being sarcastic.

"Why can't you be kind?" T.J. asked as he walked away, giving Jackson a smirk.

"You listen to me. Don't ever take that tone with me. Do you understand me? Never!" Jackson grabbed T.J.'s arm and jerked him back.

"Jackson, let him go," Ella said trying to release his grip on T.J.

"Did you hear me, Bryan?"

"Yes sir. My name is T.J. Now let me go."

Ella could feel the tension building again. This could be another anxious night. More than that, she was concerned about her son adjusting to their new family. She missed what she had with Thomas and losing her home in San Diego would break her heart. There were so many memories that she would keep close.

"Was that necessary? Did you see the look on his face? Don't put your hands on him again."

"Is that how this is going to play? You're defying me? I will not have anyone tell me what to do in my house, you got that?"

"Just don't touch my son."

"You know, I think you still miss his dead father. Good thing I'm here to take his place." He laughed as he walked back outside.

Ella tried to keep her cool but they both knew she was afraid of him. Jackson walked away looking at T.J. standing in the doorway as he watched his mother helpless. T.J. cried quietly as he walked to his room. The pain of being in this home was making him feel trapped. As long as he had Ella to carry any burdens he was feeling, he was able to manage one more day.

Early the next day, before they said goodbye to their home, Ella and T.J. stopped by the grave site of Thomas James Dawson. They were proud of the man that shaped his son into the man he could someday become. Ella would always love Thomas. She knew her son would grow up to be just like him. Ella had her arm around his shoulders as she wiped tears from her face. T.J. could do nothing but stand there and wonder what became of his family.

"You know I miss him, right T.J.?"

"Yes, I do. It felt like you were desperate to go on with your life. Jackson just fell into our lives and now it feels all wrong."

"I'll make it right. I will. This change will be what we need to fix what is wrong."

"I want to say you are right, but I don't think Jackson will ever change."

Ella placed her hands on her son's face as she thought that she could be making a bad mistake. She was doing this for T.J., but it became clearer it wasn't for anyone but Jackson. After their things were all packed in and the van drove away, T.J. pressed his face to the window looking into the park they passed. Was she there? He made a hard memory of the tree that he and Cara called theirs and wondered if he would ever see her again. She was his family even though they had a short time to be friends. It changed T.J.'s life. He would take Cara with him in his heart hoping her friendship would shape his future for the better.

22

Cara came by the tree the next day. She didn't climb it. She put her hand on the bark and imagined T.J. sitting there smiling down at her. She had been to many homes, met different people and made new friends, but he was no ordinary friend. She felt a loss she would not get over anytime soon. Standing there, she took another breath and walked slowly home.

Chapter 3

A Family at Last

Marcia Grier received a phone call from foster services for children awaiting adoption. This was news about Cara.

"We know you have been keeping Cara Sanderson with you for a few years now. We have some good news for her," the woman stated.

"What is the news?"

"Cara is being placed for adoption. We will be picking her up tomorrow to place her in her new home."

"So suddenly?"

"The family that wants her is very nice with one daughter of their own. They want the process to move quickly."

"I don't know what to say."

"Well, you are just fostering her. You knew this was temporary, right?"

"Of course. I'll be sure to let her know."

This news wasn't what Marcia expected. She had strict rules, but she was attached to Cara. When she came to the Grier's home, she was a shy little girl, confused by all the different families she stayed with. Marcia and her husband had been fostering kids for twenty years. They never could have children of their own, and adopting wasn't working out for them. It was then that they decided that giving children a good home would be healing for Marcia's empty heart. She knew that Cara had been in many homes where the environment was not ideal and could understand the emptiness Cara might feel because of not knowing her mother. Placement day came sooner than she thought. Each child that came to their home was a child that was going to be loved. But saying goodbye to those who got adopted out was hard and tearful. Marcia didn't know how Cara was going to take the news of leaving. Surprisingly, she had never been the type of child to hold resentment because of her circumstances. She managed to find delight in many of the friends she met and the parents who did their best. She coped with her own heartache by learning to draw portraits, often of what she thought her mother looked like. Cara stepped into the house to greet Marcia.

"I'm home on time, Marcia."

"I need to talk to you."

"What about?"

"I have some news for you."

"What kind of news?"

"Please sit down. I got a phone call today from the adoption agency. There is a family who adopted you. You will be leaving us tomorrow."

"Leaving? Where am I going? How far away?"

"It's not far. They live about an hour away from here. They are a nice family with a daughter. I'm sure you'll be happy."

"I don't think I'm ready to go. I've been here for so long."

"Oh, honey, we both knew we would have to say goodbye. You'll have a permanent home."

Cara started to cry and put her arms around Marcia.

"I know I didn't like the rules and I felt sad sometimes, but I liked being here."

"Well, you can write and keep in contact. It's always hard to adjust, but you can do it."

Cara reached in her backpack to share with Marcia. She wiped her tears as she pulled out a few sketches.

"I want you to have this. While I was here, I taught myself how to draw. You can have this to remember me by."

"Cara, you drew this? It's beautiful."

"It's a drawing of Lindley Park. I love that place, and it will always have a special place in my heart."

"Thank you, Cara."

"I'm going to miss you. It seems like everyone is leaving to say goodbye."

"What do you mean, dear?"

"My friend T.J. moved to San Francisco. He was the reason I was late that day. He was a good friend and I had to say goodbye. It was hard because he was going through some bad things in his home. We needed each other and now he's gone."

"Cara, I know these kinds of things are hard. You will go on to have a good life. It's in you. You have the passion to do good things."

"What about you?"

"Me? Oh, I'll be fine. Doug and I have been taking kids in for years. It's what we do. Most of them have gone on to have great lives. With that said, you will be missed the most."

Cara had to hold Marcia, not knowing what this new life was going to be like. She had to believe that Marcia was right about her adjusting to this new family.

"How about a snack?" Marcia asked.

"Okay."

"The agency will send someone over later so you can be prepared to meet your new family."

"Thank you for being the best mom."

"You are very welcome."

Cara didn't know what to think of this change. A permanent home with a family was a lot to take in. She had seen a counselor to be sure she was doing well in school and how to adjust in her home. It was suggested to keep a journal of her thoughts.

She remembered all the good times her and Marcia had while she was in her home. Like a mother, she loved to crochet and bake, always including the girls in learning how to be a homemaker. Those times when Cara fell and scraped her knees, Marcia was comforting and ready to wipe her tears and give her a bandage and hugs during bedtime with a favorite book. The other girls that slept there didn't mind that Cara needed a night light to help her feel safe. So many memories were created in this home. Now it was time to say goodbye and make new ones.

"Do you know what kind of family they are?"

"I know they love horses. You love to draw horses. That can be your new canvas."

"I suppose so."

Cara was nervous waiting for the adoption agent to arrive. She didn't know what these new people were going to be like. T.J. was on her mind, thinking about how lonely it was without him. She feared T.J. would forget about her.

"Cara, can you come in the living room. The agent is here."

"I'll be right there."

Cara was shy for the moment. She was going to learn about her new home and family. This should have been an exciting moment for her, but it was not.

"Hello, Cara. My name is Lori Paige. I am here to tell you about your new family."

"Can Marcia stay while we talk?"

"Well, I think it would be best if it was just us for now."

"I won't be here without Marcia."

"Okay, she can stay."

"I want her to feel comfortable," Marcia added.

"I agree," said the agent.

"What is the name of the family?" Cara asked.

"Saunders. They have a daughter your age. They raise horses. I heard from Marcia that you like to draw. You will find plenty to be inspired by. They live in the country."

"Cara taught herself to draw," said Marcia.

"That's wonderful. Do you have any questions for me, Cara?"

"When do I leave?"

"Tomorrow. I think you're going to like this family."

"I hope so."

After chatting for a while, Cara went to her room. Marcia followed her.

"Cara, are you okay?"

"Yes. I just need to process it. I thought I would pack my things tonight,"

"Alright. What are you feeling right now?"

"I'm going to miss you. It will be nice to be settled with a family. It's just all too new."

"You are going to do just fine. I know you miss your real mom, but you got a good start being here with us."

"Sometimes I think about finding her, but it's just a thought."

"Well, whatever you do in your life, you will do good things for yourself. You are very creative and talented. No dream is out of reach for you."

Marcia hugged Cara and she had the reassurance that she was safe and loved in the Grier home. Packing her stuffed animals, books, journals, and keepsakes, Cara was ready to take on her new journey.

Morning came and three of the children living in the home waited by the front door to say goodbye. Marcia came to Cara to give her something.

"What's this?" Cara asked

"It's a drawing set with everything you'll need to draw those horses. We all want to give this to you."

"Thank you."

The agency sent over a car to pick up Cara. As the driver was loading her things, she turned to wave goodbye. Marcia had tears in her eyes as Cara said her last words to her.

"Marcia, I love you."

"I love you too."

Cara looked out the car window not knowing what to feel. She was anxious but happy. She was going to a permanent home. As the driver pulled onto the road leading up to the house, Cara couldn't believe her eyes. The house was nestled in the countryside, with fields and open space. There were white fences bordering the property lines. Horses were grazing in the fields along with two foals near their mothers. The house was massive. A two-story home with beautifully landscaped yards. As they drove to the front of the home, there were flower beds with beautifully arranged colors, large trees, and lush green grass surrounding a large fountain. The house seemed romantically mosaic to Cara, like something out of a movie. The driver helped Cara unload her things. The agent went along to introduce her to the Saunders family.

"Well, what do you think, Cara? Are you ready to meet your new family?"

"I think I'm ready."

The agent knocked on the door. Derek Saunders came to the door to greet them.

"Well, hello Lori!"

"Hi, Derek. I'd like you to meet Cara Sanderson."

"Hello, Cara. Welcome to your new home. Come on in."

The foyer was wide, and the floors to the entry were laid with marble. There was a large antique mirror, ornate and gold hanging on the wall. The ceilings were high with dark wood beams. There was a grand piano in the living room across from the fireplace. The windows were tall, and the light loved coming into this room. Sheers of light ivory were diffusing the sunlight to soften it. Under the large area rug were rustic hardwood floors with strong grain patterns. The house had charm.

"Let's sit down and chat a bit," Derek invited.

"Is your wife going to join us?" asked Lori.

"She should be here any moment. She went with Jocelyn on her riding lesson."

"Jocelyn is their daughter," Lori explained.

"We have your room all ready for you." Derek said.

"Thank you."

Just as they were about to start their conversation, the back door opened, and Jocelyn and her mother walked in. They were wearing their riding clothes. As they removed their hats and jackets, they turned to a man dressed as a butler. Cara noticed him bringing them some beverages. She didn't say a word. Her eyes wandered around the home still amazed at the art and décor. They both walked up to Cara with their hand out to greet her. It felt formal.

"I am Mrs. Jane Saunders, and this is our daughter."

"Hi, I am Jocelyn."

"Dear, can you please join us so we can get to know our new addition to the family?" Derek asked.

Derek was a kind, gentle man. His father was a real estate investor who came from three generations of wealthy developers. Derek took over the business when his father died. He was the youngest child and after cashing in his father's stocks and bonds and inheriting his estate, Derek renovated the home he shared with Jane and Jocelyn. His wife did not come from money. She grew up on a small income and met Derek at a party. They had been married eighteen years. Their daughter Jocelyn was fourteen just like Cara.

Jocelyn was happy to see Cara. She was the obvious reason the Saunders family adopted her. She seemed lonely and lost even though she had everything a child could want. There was a sadness her parents noticed that concerned them. A counselor suggested another child in the home might help.

The family learned a little of Cara's history. They knew she was gifted in art, and she was a kind child. It might just be what the family needed.

"Mom, can I show Cara her room?" Jocelyn asked.

"Yes, you may."

"Come on, Cara. I'll show you my room too."

"She seems like a bright child," Jane remarked.

"She is very talented. It was very hard parting ways with her foster mother. Give her some time to adjust," advised Lori.

Jane couldn't wait to place Cara in the finest schools, riding lessons, and learning the arts. Derek wanted Cara to ease into her new life. Jane felt differently. She had much higher expectations for her girls.

"Mr. and Mrs. Saunders, here are the last of the papers on the adoption. I have another child to place today so I should get going. You have my number if you have questions."

"Thank you. She will be well cared for," Derek affirmed.

Jane didn't say much. Derek looked over at her to signal her to speak.

"Jane, thank Miss Paige for coming," Derek said.

"Thank you for your time, Miss Paige."

Jane briskly turned and walked away, instructing the butler to summon the chef for dinner preparations.

Jocelyn opened the door for Cara showing her the room that was prepared for her.

"Do you like it?"

"Wow, it so big. This is just for me?"

"Yes. I have my own room over there. We can have sleepovers if you want," Jocelyn said.

"You have a butler and chef?"

"Yes. My parents don't have much time to cook or do much around here. The chef comes about three or four times a week or when we have a party. It's weird but it works for them."

Cara's room was spacious with two large closets. Her bedding was patterned with a soft floral print. It was fluffy and there was lace along the bottom of it. Wallpaper rested on the wall above the headboard in a beautiful pattern of pinks, blues, and pastels. The ceilings were high and there were windows with a view of the fields and stables. A Hydrangea bush with white petals grew outside of her bedroom window. Cara didn't have many belongings and it was obvious she was overwhelmed with the amount of space.

"I don't have a lot of things."

"We can go shopping. My mother loves to shop. We can find some cute clothes for you."

"What do you do for fun, Jocelyn? Do you have a hobby or projects you like to do?"

"There are lots of things I want to do, but my mom makes me take piano and riding lessons."

"You don't like the lessons?"

"No, not really. Mother says, "I'll thank her later when I grow up." What do you like to do?"

"I like to draw. While I was in foster care, I taught myself. Would you like to see some of my art?"

"Yes."

Cara opened her bag and took out some of her favorites.

"You draw horses?"

"I love to draw animals and trees."

"I wish I could draw. I went to an art class once, it was boring. I think it's great you learned on your own."

"It helped me get my mind off of my mother."

"My father said you were left at a hospital."

"Yes, I was. I wish I could find her. No one claimed me so I just went from one foster home to another. I miss her every day."

"I always wanted a sister. Come on, I want to show you my horse. His name is Halley, like Halley's Comet."

The girls were getting along and so far, Cara liked her new home and the horses that she couldn't wait to draw. Walking toward the stables, she felt the breeze go through her hair. It had an earthy scent. The wide-open space of the countryside gave her a feeling of calm. Petting the horses put her in touch with nature. She gained inspiration from it all.

"I can't wait for us to ride together, Cara."

"I've never rode before. Are you sure I can ride a horse someday?"

"My mother will make sure you take lessons."

"What about your father?"

"He works a lot. My mother belongs to several community organizations. I started riding when I was three. It scared me at first, then I learned to love it."

"Have you ever thought about what you want to do when you finish school?"

"I'd love to travel the world, see different countries, maybe, Europe. Dad wants me to be a partner in his real estate business, you know, keep it in the family."

"Well, I think you should go for what you want."

"I love photography. I want to publish a photography book of all my travels. That's my dream."

Cara loved listening to her new sister talk about her dreams. It helped her to never give up on her own goal to become an artist. She could feel in her heart that it was going to be a good friendship, developing a closeness that only sisters have for each other. Jocelyn made her feel like she was family...finally.

Chapter 4

Who Do You Love?

The mist was coming into the city. Looking out his window, T.J. tried to see the distant buildings. He wasn't used to seeing fog from the bay. It always felt sad. He was missing the days when he had Cara to rely on. She changed his emotions and feelings. He knew he shouldn't be sad for too long. He had promised to write, and he was still looking for her letter to arrive. He had school to focus on and being there for his mother while dealing with a controlling stepfather. The thought of Cara took away the negative thoughts he had about homelife. The trees he had found close by were not the same. The neighborhood he came from was pleasant, calming, and inviting, and it seemed to come to life when he met Cara. Was she thinking of him? Would she keep her promise and write as much as she could? The home he lived in was even smaller than where they used to live. He didn't walk to school but took the bus every day. He still came home to an empty house because his parents both worked. It felt lonely to be in the new house without someone to laugh with, to talk to, to share stories about life even at fourteen. T.J. was turning fifteen the next week and his thoughts were often on his mother's happiness. She tried hard to look happy but there were moments when she cried in her room, sleeping alone. Her sister would call to make sure she was safe and okay. Ella was never the type to ask for help or for anyone to carry her burdens for her. Talking to her sister, she could feel her love and support. When she met Jackson, she was just getting over her husband Thomas' death. He was her first love and losing him to heart disease was devastating for the whole family. Jackson was caring at the time, a diligent worker and had more money than most folks. She met him while having her house remodeled. He was the contractor she hired to fix her roof and redo the kitchen. He had done a good job at concealing who he was, hiding a dark past that he tried to put behind him. She learned later that he punched a co-worker a few years ago. His past was filled with jail time, restraining orders, and the reputation of a bad temper. Ella was always kind to him during those awkward times. She was a good wife and tried her best to make the situation better. But the issues were not her problem, they were Jackson's. She knew she could not provide enough on her own. Her husband's life insurance was a small amount of money that covered the basic expenses. Ella didn't want to sell her house and move but she felt she had no better choice. Jackson insisted it was the best and only thing to do.

T.J. didn't grow up with that stressful environment before Jackson moved in. It was new to him. He had to adjust for the sake of his mother. As he was growing into a man, he wanted to think more about his future. What kind of a person was he to become to benefit him and his mother? Those choices were not easy for a teenager to think about, but he felt it was necessary to plan it out.

"T.J., did you do your homework tonight?" Ella asked.

"In a minute, Mom."

She came into his room.

"What are you doing? Is that homework?"

"No. I'm writing to my friend Cara. I really miss living in San Diego."

"I know. I miss it too. Jackson's income does help."

"You know I never cared about his money."

"I know you don't like Jackson."

"I don't have to like him. He never talks to me, and we never go out to just be together. He's nothing like Dad."

"T.J., I'm just trying to do the right thing. He's my husband and I'm trying to adjust to his personality. Sometimes I feel like there is no way out, like this was my fault. I know you miss your dad. Jackson will never replace him."

"It's late, Mom. Where is Jackson? He should have been home by now. Why does he leave you alone?"

"I don't know the answer to that question. Don't stay up too late. Try to get in some homework right after you finish your letter. Love you, T.J."

"Love you too, Mom"

Ella knew her husband wasn't the best at being a father. She remembered times when things were good between them at first and she wasn't sure what happened to them. If it were going to run its course, a goodbye could be on the way. She didn't want to believe it, but she was feeling trapped in an abusive relationship.

T.J. looked at the letter he wrote Cara. He had to finish his homework, but he wanted to write the last few words to ease his mind. He imagined reading this to her while she listened.

Dear Cara,

It's been a few weeks since we said goodbye. I am so glad I get to write you even though we are far apart. Distance doesn't scare me when I know you are alive in this world and you will receive this letter. I hate it here in San Francisco. I haven't made any friends at school and there are no trees like the one at Lindley Park. I loved climbing it with you. There were so many words I wanted to carve, especially with you there. I come home from school and I am alone. My mom must work so we can afford to stay here. Jackson never talks to me. He just seems so unhappy with everything. I don't want to be like him. I want to be there for my mom and come back to San

Diego and turn and see you at our tree and things can be like they used to be. I miss you.

Please write back soon, T.J. Bryan Dawson

Since T.J. didn't know about Cara's adoption, the letter was forwarded to her new residence. Cara received it from the butler and running to her room she eagerly opened it, anticipating his words. After she read his letter aloud, she grinned and held the paper to her chest. She put the letter in her drawer. Every teenage girl should get letters like that. To Cara, this was someone she was drawn to, he was special. She thought of what she would write back to him. She didn't care if it sounded poetic, she just wanted it to be sincere. At that moment, she heard Jane at her door.

"Cara, can you please come out to the living room?"

"I'll be right out."

Cara came out to talk to her new parents.

"Cara, sit down," Jane said, frankly.

"Is something wrong?"

"No. We need to talk about some things. As you know we are a family of successors. We have worked very hard getting Jocelyn into the finest schools and lessons in the arts. We are prepared to enroll you in equestrian lessons just like Jocelyn. Also, we will be starting you in piano lessons first thing next week."

Jane was making herself clear and she wasn't going to take no for an answer.

"I really don't need any of those things. I like going to public school and drawing in my free time."

"This is not negotiable. This is how it's going to be. This will help you get a good start out there in the real world," Jane said more forcefully.

"Why do I need that to be successful? I don't mean to sound disrespectful."

"We know you are being open with your feelings, and I think..." Derek started.

"You have no say in this young lady. You will report to the trainer on Monday and start your first riding lesson. Have I made myself clear?"

"I heard what you said. I don't agree with it. I believe that I should choose."

"Well, you are just a child. You don't know what's best for you."

"Jane, that's enough."

Derek was disturbed by Jane's words and placed his hand on her forearm.

Cara bowed her head and said, "I'm going to my room now."

"You don't leave until you are excused," Jane demanded.

"Cara, you may leave," Derek said warmly.

Jane just sat there looking away as Derek spoke.

"What was that? How could you speak to her like that? She's been our daughter for just a few weeks, and you spring that on her."

"You don't think for a minute I have her interests at heart? Jocelyn will thank us later for introducing her to the more important things in life. We should want that for Cara."

"Have you even asked Jocelyn if that is what she wants?"

"It's not up to her. We are her parents!"

"You don't have to remind me of that. Have you noticed how happy Jocelyn has been since getting to know Cara? This was why we wanted her to be part of our family."

"These girls are going to do better in the best schools out there because of..."

"Because of what? You? You can't always force others to see things your way!"

"Cara is going to take her riding lessons and that's it. I am going to do it my way. We're done, Derek."

Jane walked out leaving Derek feeling helpless. Cara wasn't his natural daughter, but he knew she needed to be herself. He treated her like his own. He respected where she came from and wanted to honor her wishes to make her own choices. It was out of his hands because so many times Derek tried to do what was best for Jocelyn, but Jane became the aggressor, forcing things and making their marriage difficult. Jane was going to do what she wanted. Derek thought it was best to go to Cara's room to talk to her. He could hear her sobs through the door.

"Cara, it's Derek. Can we talk?"

She opened the door partway.

"Hey, can I come in?" he asked.

"Sure."

"I'm sorry about Jane. She is used to taking charge when it comes to her daughter."

"I don't want to take any lessons."

"I know. They are not your favorite subjects. I have a favor to ask. Can you give it a chance? At least for a while? I heard you tell Jocelyn you liked horses. You might enjoy riding and you can ride with Jocelyn. Will you give it a try?"

"What about what I want to do?"

"What do you want to do? What do you want to be when you are an adult?"

"An artist or an architect."

"Well, who says you can't be that? Riding horses or playing piano can't take that goal away from you, right?"

"I guess it can't hurt."

"What are you thinking?"

"I'm afraid of Jane."

"No, she's harmless. She just wants the best for our family. I don't always agree with her on some of her ideas. But we can always try it out."

"Okay. I can do that."

"Go find Jocelyn and let her know dinner will be ready soon."

He smiled at her then turned to go back downstairs.

"Thank you, Derek."

"You're welcome. I like having you as a daughter."

Cara smiled when he said that.

It was clear that Cara was going to have to do what Jane wanted. Derek was a loving father. He has always had mixed emotions about Jane and the way she aggressively took over the household. As a father, he would also have to talk with Jocelyn. He knew she had been unhappy for a while, and she still felt alone. He saw her smile returning when the girls played together. Derek was disturbed with his wife being so overbearing. He wanted peace in his family, and he knew Jane loved to be deeply involved with local events and was a big part of the equestrian club her daughter was in. Derek loved Jane but he needed to let her know that his feelings about what the girls needed was equally important.

Cara and Jocelyn helped do the dishes after dinner. It was Derek's one allowance meant to keep his girls grounded in the real-world of manual labor. With soapy hands, Cara proceeded to tell Jocelyn about how her mother was starting her lessons.

"Yep, I told you. I have been riding for years and I wanted to quit several times and she always said no. When I'm older, I'm off to Europe."

"I like your dad. He made me feel better about being here and dealing with Jane. Besides, we can ride together once I get good at it."

"Hey, he's your dad too."

"He is, isn't he? I like how that sounds."

That night, Cara started to write her letter to T.J. She didn't know where to start since so much had happened. By night lamp in her pajamas, she took out her notepad.

Dear T.J.,

You started off with "dear," so I did too. I liked your letter. I miss the park too. I got adopted and my new family is rich. They have horses and lots of property for riding. I must take riding lessons and go to private school. I don't like it, but Derek, my new dad, says I should just go with it for now.

How is your mom? I was thinking about how I wish Jackson would just go away and you can come back to San Diego. Let's hope you come back soon. You know, even though you're not there anymore, the tree will always be there with our initials. I will be just like that tree. No matter what, I will always be there. Even though my adopted parents have money, it doesn't mean that I

43

want to be that way. I still want to be an artist. Do you think when I'm older I will still want to climb trees? What a funny thought! I know we both will.

When you get sad, do you think about the last time we were together? Close your eyes. Wasn't that a great time for us? That is what I think of when I miss you. I will write as much as I can. They keep me busy here. Thank you, my friend, Cara

Chapter 5

Run with the Horses

Ten years had gone by since Cara was adopted. She is now twenty four. Cara worked hard to win blue ribbons for excellence in jumping and dressage. She learned about farriers and proper horse care. Being proficient, she had high expectations for herself based on her new and well-practiced talent. She grew to love riding and with experience, she used her craft as a way to gain confidence. Jane pushed her into it and Derek encouraged her to fall in love with it. She could never pursue it professionally. Jane did not agree, wanting Cara to be the best rider of the sport. She wanted her to be competitive and that was not Cara's way. Her horse, Kindred, was trained by the finest trainers available.

Jocelyn had her first-place wins in her younger days when she was a preteen. But things were changing for her. Jocelyn was thinking about her goals to go to Europe. She had been taking local photographs professionally for a while. She met with Xander Haught, who worked for a publishing company specializing in photography books. Her talent was obvious to them, and they were interested. Jocelyn didn't know how she was going to tell her mother she was leaving on an assignment. She knew there would be strong disagreement. She had her father's blessing. As he looked at her pictures each week, he was impressed and told her how proud he was. She was twenty four and had the drive to go for her dream.

Jane had been away with her assistant searching for specialty horses to raise and breed. She was used to getting her way and would get the horses she wanted no matter what the price. When she returned, Jocelyn was making plans to tell her mother her news. Coming from her bedroom she saw Jane in the kitchen.

"How was your trip, Mom?"

"It went very well. There is a horse I purchased for you. We are retiring Halley. I'm selling him to a nice family who wants an older horse."

"I've had Halley for years. Didn't you think to ask me whether he should be sold or not? You can't give him away!"

"It's important that you know you are just the rider. You won competitions and after a few years, we have to go with a younger horse."

"Did you forget I'm no longer competing? He was like my best friend. I never thought you would do such a thing."

"Nonsense! Where is this attitude coming from? We discussed this subject many times. He is sold and that's it. They are coming to get him in the morning. I suggest you say your goodbye soon."

"You are so cruel! I love Halley. Don't let them take him."

"It's too late. Again, we agreed on this."

"No, you discussed it many times. I never agreed to that. Why do you need to take control of everything? Does Father have anything to say about your ways?"

"I don't have to answer that."

"Yes, you do."

Jocelyn showed it in her voice that she was tired of her mother using her force to get what she wanted. Jane's expression was less than pleased by her questioning.

"When you go into the world, you will be glad you learned everything from me. You are being very ungrateful."

"I'm ungrateful? You are pushing Cara and I into what you want, and it isn't fair to either of us. Well, right now it ends."

"What are you saying?"

"I've already talked about it with Dad and I'm leaving for Europe on Tuesday. A publisher wants me to do a book on the European Countryside and I'm doing it. I never wanted to do any of those things you thought were good for me. They are not really who I am!"

"Your father never told me you wanted to leave. Is he giving you the money to go?"

"Of course. I'm leaving whether you think it's right or not!"

"So, everything I did for you was a waste? Fine, go throw away your life."

"That's not what I'm doing. Who have you become?"

"You mentioned Cara. What does she have to do with this? Did she influence your decision?"

"Cara is not your natural daughter. You made sure she became a winner in your competitions, so it looked like you won."

"Because of what I did, she did become a winner."

"No, she did all the work. All you did was pressure her into something she had no control over. Have you spoken to her? She wants to be an artist and go to an architectural school."

"That's absurd."

"That is what you think! I was hoping you would be proud of us, but now I can't even look at you anymore," Jocelyn turned, "How could this have happened?" she wondered aloud.

Jane could do nothing but stand there stunned by the conversation that took place. That was not what she planned for.

Jane married into money. She met Derek when she was doing a ball charity for Cancer Awareness. She was tall and lovely to look at. Derek came to her table to introduce himself. Standing outside together looking at the sunset, they drank champagne and talked about what supporting the charities meant to her. She never had much money of her own. Instead, she was in charge of raising funds for good causes. After seeing each other romantically for a year, they were married. At that time, Jane decided that never again would she be without. She would ensure that her children would never struggle like her. She was well taken care of by Derek and his wealth. It made her feel important. Their love was put on hold when her power became too much for her husband to manage. Derek was still in love and getting through to his wife became less easy. He was generous and kind to her and since the girls would be pursuing other adventures, he was thinking it was time to get his wife back.

Jocelyn went out to the stables. She was crying as she looked into the eyes of her dear horse. She kissed him and her tears were on his hide. She knew he could sense her sadness. She wanted to find Cara. She brushed him and put her horse back in its stable when she looked up.

"Hey, what's wrong?" Cara asked.

"I did it. I told her I'm leaving." Jocelyn was trying to calm her urge to cry.

"Oh no. I take it from the look on your face she didn't like it."

"No, she didn't. I could never understand what my father saw in her."

"Oh, come on. I'm sure she wasn't like that when she met your dad. There has to be a reason she's so strong about everything."

"She's selling Halley."

"Oh, Jocelyn, I'm so sorry."

"Before you came, he was the only friend I had to talk to. I know that seems weird, but..."

"I know what you mean. I had a few of those moments growing up in foster homes."

"He's going to a ranch that apparently likes older horses."

"How are you feeling now that you told her?"

"It didn't go like I planned but that's on her. I wanted her to be proud of me. I built my photography business on my own and with Dad's help. It is my dream."

Cara put her arm on her shoulder, "I'm going to miss you, Jocelyn. I know you have to do what makes you happy."

"So do you. When was the last time you got a letter from T.J.?"

"It's been a while. Lately his letters have been shorter and coming once every few months."

It became quiet and Jocelyn could see she was perplexed.

"You know, as we grow up, things change. I've changed and so have you. All you can do is hope for the best. Have you been writing to him even when you don't get a letter?"

"I have, but I am losing hope and I'm afraid we've lost touch. I never wanted that to happen. I promised him."

"Remember when we had that conversation when we were kids, what we were going to do when we graduated? We're here now and I think you should go for your dream too. If T.J. lost touch with you, you may have to move on from that. Don't lose your desire to pursue your career too."

"I wish you were there when we were kids. He went through a lot in his home. He missed his father after he died, and his stepfather made life miserable for him. He needed me."

49

"Things will get better soon. Are you excited to start architectural school?"

"Yes. Dad enrolled me for the Fall semester."

"Hey, I promised to keep in touch. That's a guarantee you can count on. Unlike the promises my mom keeps."

"I know you love her. She loves you too. Marcia, my foster mom, used to say, "Parents sometimes hold on too tight for fear their children may fail." She might not want to let go."

"Well, my dad is happy for me."

"So am I."

That day the sisters bonded stronger than ever. Each was taking control of their lives. Cara didn't show it much, but her determination was internal, and she knew what made her the happiest. She saved every one of T.J.'s letters. She missed him but needed to focus on college. In her heart, she knew school wasn't forever. That was a memory that would always stay with her. Cara expected Jane to blame her for her daughter leaving.

Derek was in his office when Jane approached him.

"I just had a talk with Jocelyn!"

"Oh? What about?"

She pointed at him, "You know what about. How dare you give her your permission to go to Europe! She's only twenty four. She needs to go to school where it will benefit her future, not running around Europe by herself!"

"You mean where it benefits you, Jane. We both knew our girls were going to take control of their own careers someday. Jocelyn will be twenty five soon and she will be well taken care of in Europe by her publishers. This is the career she has been waiting for. Do you know how hard it was for her to come to you? She wanted you to be happy for her."

"I worked so hard to get her to where she is. Cara had something to do with this. I can feel it."

Cara was walking by and overheard the conversation.

"Excuse me, did I hear you right? Do you really think I helped Jocelyn make her decision? Why would you say that?"

"I don't think she meant that, Cara," Derek countered as he looked at Jane.

"Oh, I meant that. She tells me you are also making your own career choice."

"Of course, I am. I did what you asked when you asked me to take piano and riding lessons. I won your blue ribbons and became the best at doing what you wanted. Now it's my turn to run with the horses. I can now be free to make my choice."

Jane walked up close to Cara and looked her in the face.

"You listen to me, Cara Jo. You had no right to influence my daughter."

"Jane, that's enough. Cara, will you please leave the room while I talk to Jane."

"Goodnight." Cara hugged Derek.

"Jane, I have had it with your control issues. It is going to be just you and I once the girls leave. This is about us, our marriage. I love you but this has to stop."

"I thought if I made Jocelyn love everything that I loved, she couldn't fail!"

"What makes you think she will fail? How is she going to learn? You were being a little unfair to her. What you did was not necessary. Taking it out on Cara wasn't right

51

either. She was the best thing for our daughter, and you know it."

Jane refused to look at Derek.

"Jane, I want you to think about where this is going for us, you and me. Don't you want better for us? Please, think about that. I also suggest you spend some time with the girls before they leave."

Jane walked out. She felt like a failure and her marriage was in trouble. She realized Jocelyn was going away and would not be attending any of her schools to further her education.

Derek had the idea to adopt a young girl for Jocelyn and hoped it would help his wife to draw closer as a family. The problems in their marriage were there long before Cara arrived. She was stubborn in her heart and had difficulty bonding with her own daughter. Jocelyn desperately needed Jane to be her mother.

Jane planned to travel abroad for a few weeks to their vacation home. She was in her room packing bags. She called the limo to take her to the airport. After calling for her, Derek walked around the house to find her. Since their conversation, she was very quiet.

"What are you doing?" Derek asked.

"What does it look like I'm doing? I'm leaving."

"That's not necessary. Where are you going?"

"I'm staying at the chalet. Derek, I know you brought Cara here to patch things up with me. But she's the one who is turning Jocelyn against me."

"No, she's not! Jocelyn hasn't smiled this much in a very long time. Cara was the best thing for her. Now she wants to go after her dream, and you won't even talk to her."

"I had a dream too, Derek. To give my daughter the best life. Now she wants to be a photographer in Europe like a nomad. It's obvious I failed. I failed her and, according to you, I'm failing us."

"Jane, don't leave, please. I need you to be on my side, by my side. Reconsider your plans, I beg you."

Derek was saddened to see her running away instead of mending her relationships. Jane walked up to Derek to face him. She looked at his eyes and briefly caressed his cheek with her hand.

"I'm sorry. I can't do this right now."

Jocelyn heard the limo drive up to the house. She was brushing the horses when she saw her mother having bags put into the car. Jocelyn ran as fast as she could to talk to her.

"Mom, Mom, wait!"

"Jocelyn, don't make this harder than it is."

"What do you mean? Where are you going? I'm leaving in three days and you're going away? I wanted to talk to you, I want to talk about my plans. You can't go now!"

"You have already made up your mind to do your own thing. Let me do mine. I need time to think about who I am around here."

"Oh, I see. This is about you. Never mind that I am your only daughter and you just cast me aside like a stranger. How could you do this to me and Dad?"

"Cara is the stranger in this house, and she is your father's choice.

Jocelyn started crying as if begging Jane with her tears.

"Jocelyn, you are my daughter, but this goes deeper than you know."

"This is so selfish! How can you treat me like this and just leave? This is the last conversation we will have before I go. How dare you!"

"Well, I guess those can be your final words."

She got into the limo as Jocelyn ran to find her father. Jane refused to look back.

"Dad, Dad!" Jocelyn cried out.

"Jocelyn, my sweet Jocelyn. I know it hurts. I tried to convince her to stay. Where is Cara?"

"She's minding the horses."

Cara was watching outside of the barn as Jocelyn cried trying to talk to Jane. It broke her heart that she had a natural mother and father, yet everything still seemed broken in their family. Cara walked into the house to clean up. She could hear Derek talking to his daughter.

After emotions calmed down, Jocelyn came out and found Cara in the kitchen.

"I'm sure you saw what happened," Jocelyn sighed.

"I did and I'm so sorry."

"She just left. My father said he knew it was going to happen but not this soon."

"She'll be back."

"I don't know if she will come back. If she does, I won't be here. I'm leaving and she didn't even say goodbye."

Jocelyn fell into Cara's arms crying missing those times Jane used to comfort her before she became distant.

Derek planned to hire a full-time handler to tend to the horses and stalls. The girls were not able to help take care of the horses as before. Cara planned to live at home part-time and her upcoming studies would keep her busy.

The girls spent most of their time together before they had to part ways. Cara found a true friend and sister in Jocelyn.

"What actually happened between you and your mom? Why are you both having these problems?" Cara inquired.

"She had a very hard life as a child. She was raised by her grandmother. They never had much money or stability. Mom was working as a fundraiser when Dad met her. She always loved to give to the communities, and she started her own business helping entrepreneurs become more successful. Her and Dad started coming apart when she got too busy to care about us. When I talked to her about my goals, she walked away and made it clear I was not in charge of my future. We haven't been the same since."

"I always thought I would like to have my mom here so we could fight with each other," Cara said jokingly.

"It's not all it's cracked up to be. We did like the same things. I loved riding horses for fun. She used to ride with me when I was young, but only to make sure I was doing it right. I wanted it to be more about a connection between us, not a chore."

"I don't think she likes me," Cara said.

"No, don't think that. She has her own issues to deal with."

The next day, the handlers came to take Halley to his new home. Cara held Jocelyn as she watched the horse she helped raise since he was a young foal, leave her sight. She ran up to the horse one last time.

"Please, may I say goodbye?"

"Of course, Miss."

"I'll miss you, old friend. I know you loved me. We have history, you and me. Take care, Halley."

Jocelyn's heart was broken. How her mother could do that to her was past cruelty. There was nothing anyone could do to make Halley stay. She watched as they drove away with the dust following behind the trailer. Cara felt her soul sink into despair watching her sister's world collapse. She was a good support for her sister.

The next day, it was time for Jocelyn to take the first steps in being on her own.

"Are you ready to leave?"

"All packed. I'm really going to miss you. These past years getting to know you has been the best in my life." She was still sad about losing her horse.

"I'm honored."

Both could give each other what their mothers could not. Jocelyn could go with confidence and pursue her dreams and be proud of her efforts and strengths.

The time came to say goodbye to her loving father. Derek sent a car and he helped load her luggage.

"Well, this is it, Dad. I'm nervous and excited."

"You'll do fine, dear. Call me when you land no matter how late it is." She hugged him tightly as he kissed her cheek.

"I will."

"Sis, I'll be out looking for your first published photo book."

"I'll sign the first copy for you." Jocelyn's eyes welled up with tears.

They hugged tightly and Cara was moved to tell Jocelyn something she had been holding back.

"Jocelyn, I really love you."

"I love you too."

Derek wrapped his arm around Cara as they waved goodbye. He thought about how Jane missed seeing their daughter grow to be a woman with a mission to be good at what she loved. Derek for the moment was alone. He didn't know how long his wife was going to be away. He hoped the trip would change her mind and bring her back to the man who loves her.

Chapter 6

Is it Really You?

Derek thought Jane would return after a few weeks, but she had not even called. He kept busy with several new projects and spent time finding someone who loved horses with the experience needed to care for them. Cara would drive to and from school to be at home with Derek and meet the new handler.

Studying architecture was not as easy as Cara thought. There was a lot to remember. Her mind kept occupied from the time her sister and Jane left the month before. Derek had traveled to Washington to help a friend develop a piece of property. Cara was by herself and pulled out some of the letters T.J. wrote. She began to read them again. With a need to focus on her endeavors, the thought of him was still on her mind. There was one letter that made her cry when she read it. She took it out of its envelope again. She didn't care if the letter was from years ago. It had a deep meaning to her. Would she be surprised when she went to the mailbox? Would it say why he stopped writing? Cara read his words to herself.

Cara, I have been so sad without you here. I remember when we said we would always write, and I kept my promise. My mother wants me to be happy here in San Francisco, but the truth is, I am not. It is so different here and the trees are not the same because you are not here. If we climbed a new tree together, then it might be special, and I wouldn't feel so alone. I love to read your poems and letters. School has been so hard because it's not easy to make friends in a new place. Jackson was gone for a few days, and we didn't know where he was. When my mom approached him about it, he got angry and flipped the table over and she was in the corner crying. As I went to defend her, he threw me down and I sprained my wrist. I didn't call the police because I was too scared, of what I really don't know. All I thought about was rescuing my mom from this awful man. He has money but no love. I promised my mom I would never be that kind of person. We are all we have. She means everything to me and so do you. If I were old enough, I would ask you to be my girlfriend. Would you say yes? What if you said no? So many thoughts going through my mind. I'm only sixteen and I'm carrying a weight bigger than I can handle. If you were here, some of the sadness would go away but I would still be holding on to the hope everything will be okay. I will keep writing when I can but if I stop, don't judge me. It would be a good reason if I lost touch with you. I hope that is never the truth with us. I'm happy you get to ride horses and you live in the country. I wish I were there with you, and you could teach me how to ride. Take care and I will always miss you.

Bryan Dawson T.J.

It always brought back those emotions because she felt helpless that years ago she couldn't do anything to help. She worried about him, thinking of a reason he would stop writing. He mentioned he would keep writing but after she sent many letters to him, she gave up. Cara put it back with the other treasured writings from the one she could never get out of her heart.

Derek called to let Cara know the new handler was planning to come by to see the stables and horses the next morning. The hired handler's name was Jaime. She was an experienced rider and veterinarian's assistant and collaborated with farriers learning the trade. She wasn't young, but she could be trusted to do the job well. Jaime came highly recommended. Cara was prepared to meet her and welcome her to their family.

When she arrived, Cara had already been riding early that morning. After putting her horse to rest up, she saw Jaime.

"Hi, are you Jaime?" Cara asked.

"Yes, you must be Cara."

"My dad is out of town, so he asked me to escort you to the stables. I heard you have a great history with horses."

"Well, it was a hobby at first, but I just fell in love with them."

"Would you like to see where we keep them?"

"I would love that."

Walking to the stables, Cara was excited to learn more about their horses from Jaime. As she grew up, she appreciated the lessons and education she picked up from professionals.

"We only have six horses right now. We used to have eight, but my mom sold them to get younger ones. Jane may be getting more later. She sold Jocelyn's best horse."

"Oh, that's sad."

"My sister was upset because he was her best friend."

"Where is your sister now?"

"She's in Europe on a photo shoot for the year. She is a photographer. She still misses Halley."

"Horses are like family to me. I get attached, so if someone took my horse, it would be like taking my best friend away. Your dad said your mom is away on business."

"She's my adopted mom. We don't know when she will be back. Anyway, you know what to do, right? My dad should be home next week."

They walked the grounds and stables while Jaime checked the horses and tack.

"Thank you for introducing me to your horses. I'll take good care of them."

"I know you will. If you need anything, let me know. I have been busy studying to be an architect."

"That's interesting. How did you choose that career?"

"I love to draw. I taught myself when I would think about my mother. Drawing and creating helped me cope with the sadness."

"I'm sorry you had to deal with that being so young."

"I'm okay with it now. Derek is a good dad. The best a girl could have."

"It's good that you have him in your life."

"Yes, it is."

As Cara walked away, she turned to ask Jaime a question.

"Jaime, would it be okay to just talk, you and me sometime? It's nice to talk to another woman, to make sense of life."

"Sure. I want to help any way I can."

Cara smiled knowing she had a potential friend in Jaime.

Sitting at her desk, Cara received a FaceTime from Jocelyn.

"Hey Sis! What a surprise. How are you?"

"Hey, Cara. I'm in England. It is so cold right now and beautiful. We were at a ranch with cows in these green fields. It is so lovely."

"Lovely? Are you British now?"

"You do get the accent the more you are around the culture."

"I haven't heard from you lately."

"We've been traveling. I talked to Dad, and he said we have a new handler for the horses. Do you like her?"

"Yes. She's very nice, a real professional."

"I didn't want to ask about Mom. Is she back yet?"

"No. She hasn't even called. I think Dad has been wrapped up in work to avoid thinking about her."

"I miss her too. It's hard for me to talk about her since we left on bad terms. I'm hoping to come for a visit in six months. I'll let you know exactly when I will arrive."

"That would be fantastic!"

"I gotta go. Hug Dad for me. Miss you so much."

"Miss you more."

"Bye."

That made Cara's heart so happy to hear that her sister was doing well. She didn't want to admit that her family was broken. She wanted to believe that Jane would return, and Derek would get his wife back. The weeks sped by, and Derek returned home. The house always felt friendlier with him in it. School was going on break soon and Cara wanted to visit her old neighborhood while on vacation. Derek thought it would be a good idea too.

"Are you going to visit Marcia?" he asked.

"I was thinking about it. There is a special place I liked to go when I was a kid, Lindley Park. There is a tree there that reminds me of someone I used to know."

"A favorite childhood memory?"

"Yes. I'll only be gone for a few days."

"Drive safely. Oh, by the way, how did you like the new handler?"

"I like her. I think it's great she is a horse lover. That makes her job easy."

"She's doing a good job. I'm glad you like her."

"How have you been? Have you tried to call Jane?"

"I got tired of leaving voicemails," Derek admitted.

"Are you sure I should go? You might need some company."

"No. You worked hard, and you need this break. I reserved a nice bed and breakfast nearby that you are going to love."

"If you want me to come home early, call me."

"Of course. Have fun."

Cara saw Jaime riding toward the house.

"Hi Jaime. It's late. Are you going home soon?"

"Well, I asked Derek if I could ride the new horse. It's relaxing for me and good for her too."

"Great. I'm leaving for San Diego now. I'll see you when I get home."

"Have a nice trip."

"Thank you."

Cara anticipated her trip to Lindley Park. She hadn't seen the tree since she moved away. Feelings for T.J. were stronger than she realized. She felt empty missing what they once had. She loved driving through her old neighborhood. The architecture was inspiring at the city's skyline. It gave her ideas for future designs she could create. She loved what she was learning but reserved a special place in her heart for her art. Canvases and acrylic paints with an array of colors to draw so many different images were what she adored. In her spare time, she would sit in the barn and draw Jocelyn standing next to the horse she no longer had. This trip was a time of reflection. Those childhood memories seemed like yesterday.

She drove to the Grier home, hoping to see Marcia. Walking up to the door, Cara was excited. The steps to the front door seemed smaller. This home had left a positive impression on her. She recalled little things that happened there. Marcia made her home a wonderful place to grow up.

"Hello?" she peered through the opening.

"Hello, Marcia. It's me, Cara."

"Cara. Oh, my I am so glad to see you. You are all grown up. Please come in."

"Are you still fostering kids?"

"No. I got too old to carry the babies. I couldn't keep up with the mess. What are you doing here in town?"

"I'm on break. I'm going to architectural school. It's my first year. It's amazing how much math you have to learn."

"I remember you talked about how much you loved art. Buildings can be artistic."

"I still draw. I will never give that up."

"How is your adopted family?"

"They're okay. My sister went to Europe. Derek and I have connected as father and daughter. I really love my family."

"What about the mother? Do you get along with her?"

"I don't quite know what she thinks of me. She is away for a while. She separated from Dad I guess to clear her head.

After Jocelyn went abroad, we hired a horse handler to help around the ranch."

"I'm sorry to hear about your parent's troubles. You like the horses?"

"Oh, yes. I took riding lessons for a few years."

"Wow, look at you. All grown up and you survived. Remember, sweetie, all families have their issues. Jane will come around."

"The real reason why I came here is because I miss someone I was close to when I lived here."

"I hope it was me," Marcia chuckled.

"Of course. Do you remember the day I came home late and you punished me? That was the day I made friends with a boy who climbed that big tree at Lindley Park."

"You loved that place."

"I will always love it. We made a promise to write and never forget each other."

"Oh, honey, young people can't keep promises. Things change so much when you grow up."

"You are probably right. Lately I have been thinking about him. A few years ago, he stopped writing. I feel like something went wrong."

"You did nothing wrong. He could have had a good reason."

"I guess I came here wishing to find him, hoping he might have moved back or something hopeful."

"What are you feeling right now?"

"I think I love him. I don't really know him anymore. I'm not sure what to do."

"You're doing your best. Keep having faith that he may decide to write again."

The two women talked about Cara's childhood, laughing about the good times. Marcia never forgot all the children that she helped mold and shape into fine adults. Cara was no exception. So many people had touched her life. As an adult, she could see challenges before her. After saying goodbye, Cara decided to go to the park.

It was chilly outside. It was misty early in the day and the benches were still wet. She walked down the path past joggers and a small group gathering for their soccer game. She could hear the rustling leaves. The tree that brought back so many memories had little foliage. She started to become melancholic as she looked at all the names carved into the bark. Was she too old to climb it again? Placing her hands around the branch, she pulled herself up. Maneuvering to the top where her and T.J. once perched, she observed something she had not seen before. The initials B.D. were carved next to hers. He must have added that when he was alone. More than ever, Cara wanted to find him. What if he didn't live in San Francisco anymore? What if he got married? She had all these thoughts running through her mind. It was a good time to check into her B and B.

The next day she awoke in her cozy room. The sun was out and the view outside her window was beautiful. She planned to walk around the beachside after breakfast, but her plans kept pulling her back to Lindley. It made her smile to remember happy times playing with the other children and sketching. As she sat on the bench, elderly women would smile at her as they strolled by. Did they have the same memories?

Stepping out of the Bed and Breakfast on her third day, she stopped by the park again. It was important to take a picture of their tree. Walking toward it, she glanced at a man in a black suit sitting on the bench. His hands were on his face. Why would anyone be in a black suit on such a warm day? Her curiosity motivated her to sit on the other end. He was looking at the ground. From the side, he looked handsome but worried and in deep thought. Cara felt bold enough to talk to this stranger.

"It's a warm day today," Cara started.

"It is."

"Do you work nearby?" she asked.

"Why would you ask that?"

"You're wearing a suit in this heat. I don't know a lot of people who dress so formal on a sunny day."

"Well, to answer you, no. I'm not working near here. I just got back from a funeral."

"Oh, I'm sorry. Was it someone you were close to?"

"Yes, my mother."

"Do you want to be alone? I didn't mean to disturb you. I just wanted to be sure you were feeling all right."

Cara stood up to leave and then added, "I used to come here as a kid. This place makes me feel good. I met my best friend here. I saw you feeling sad, and it seemed like you needed a friend too."

"It's okay. You can stay. I mean, it's a free park. No charge to use the bench. If you must know, I used to live here too."

She sat back down, "A lot of good times. Did your mother live here?"

"She moved back here when her marriage fell apart."

"Was she sick?"

"Yes. About a year ago she fell sick with cancer. I took care of her until she passed. There was no one like her. She deserved more than life gave her. She went through so much and now I'm here at this park because this is where I was the happiest."

"Why was that?" She asked because this sounded too familiar.

"I met someone here when I was a kid. She stayed on my mind, and I missed her so much after I moved away."

Cara felt her heartbeat as he talked about familiar memories. He started to relax, as if he trusted her talking about his life and why he came to the park.

"Can I ask what your name is?"

"I'm Bryan, I mean, T.J."

Cara couldn't believe that she was sitting next to the man who changed her life. She had to catch her breath. She didn't know what to do. Realizing that she was sitting next to someone she loved was not how she expected it. What were the odds that he would be here? That was her wish. She stood up and took a few steps away. She decided not to tell him who she was. The shock may have been too much. She felt flustered and happy at the same time.

"Are you okay?" he asked.

"Oh, yes." She felt nervous knowing this was T.J.

"It's nice to meet you, Bryan." She held out her hand.

"Please, call me T.J."

"I know we just met and I'm not sure if you want to, but would you like to meet again here tomorrow?"

"Why? You don't know me."

"You seem harmless. Besides, it's nice to talk to someone who grew up here and likes this place as much as I do. So, what do you say, can you come back?"

Cara was waiting for his answer.

"I can come back. Wait, you didn't tell me your name."

She was walking back to her car, and she turned and shouted, "I'll see you tomorrow around 11 o'clock in the morning."

The smile on Cara's face was expressing the happiness she was feeling. She was talking to T.J. How was she going to reveal herself to him? She didn't want to scare him away. All those years, she thought about him, reading his letters over and over. It was like a lost fairy tale. He was actually at the park, their park, and her heart was glad he was alive.

The next day, Cara spotted him sitting at the bench. He was not dressed so formally.

"Hi, you made it," Cara said.

"I thought I'd sit at the same place so you could find me."

"Since your mother lived here, did you move back here to help her out?"

"No. I stayed in San Francisco. I came to see her often and helped her with money. I work for a marketing company where I manage a few employees. I had to take time off work to help her during her treatments."

"When do you have to go back home?"

"Tomorrow. I was going to leave today but you asked me to stay. We're both from here so I thought, why not?"

"This person who you knew when you were young, who was it?"

"It was a girl. Her name was Cara Sanderson. We both lost someone we loved when we were young, and she felt like my family. I didn't know her very long, but it made a big impact on my life."

"Did you love her?"

"I guess I did. I was fourteen at the time. She was special. I broke my promise to her."

"What was it?"

Cara was drawn to him as she listened to him speak. His voice was quite manly.

"I stopped writing her when my mom got really sick. I was in my head and couldn't think about anyone but Mom."

Cara stood up. Looking away she nervously wiped her eyes. She needed to say something, she needed to reveal her identity.

"Excuse me, are you okay?" he asked.

"There's something I need to tell you, Bryan."

"What is it? I hope I haven't said something to make you uncomfortable."

"No, you haven't done anything wrong. I need to tell you something. I had doubts about it yesterday, but it has become clear to me."

He walked over to her and looked into her eyes. "Would that be your name? You never did tell me what it is."

Cara was afraid to tell him who she was. She looked at his face, the face she remembered so many years ago. She felt her flushed cheeks because of the overflow with emotion.

"My name is Cara Sanderson."

T.J. took a breath and put his hands through his hair.

"Cara? This is impossible." He turned away for a moment and walked back over to her, looking into her eyes.

"I wrote you a poem and gave you the note before you moved to San Francisco. Your mother's name was Ella, and your stepdad was Jackson."

"Tell me what the poem said." He sat back on the bench. It wasn't that he didn't believe her, he wanted to hear her recite what she wrote to him.

"I can't remember it word for word. It goes like this,

When you meet someone special

Even though you must go away

I will never forget you

Cara

I may have misquoted it but…"

"No, you got most of it right. I'm awestruck that it is you. This can't be happening. And you're sitting right in front of me. I thought about you every day. I missed you. There were so many times I just wanted to run away to find you."

"I came here hoping to rekindle our memories and had a thought that by some miracle I would find you. I have never stopped thinking about you."

"I never let you out of my heart. I'm sorry I stopped writing."

"No, it doesn't matter now. I'm glad you're here. I saved all your letters. I've read them so many times. T.J., I think I'm in love with you."

T.J. took her hand as she stood there to face him. His arms wrapped around her and held her tightly. They were making up for years apart. They were softly tearing up because they knew this meeting was so surreal. He was grieving for his mother. She was longing for his love.

"What should we do now? I have to be back in school tomorrow."

He put his hands on her shoulders and stepped back. Softening his voice, he said, "I want to see you again. I don't ever want to lose you."

71

"You won't lose me. I have so much to tell you. These last ten years I've had you on my mind. I wanted to be in love with you even if you didn't love me."

"I was afraid you would hate me for not writing. I was too depressed to think you would even still care about me."

"I never gave up hope. You said if you stopped writing, there was a good reason. You didn't intentionally shut me out of your heart. I know you cared for me."

"So much has happened, good and bad. I was overwhelmed with so many emotions I couldn't cope or love anything."

"What happened to Jackson?" she asked. They both sat down, and he held on to her hand.

"He left and took everything. We came home after being out for the day and all our belongings were gone."

"What made him leave?"

"My mom wanted him to stay home more. She asked him not to yell at me. He got angry and left that night. I haven't seen him since. She moved back to San Diego, then she got sick. My mother died not having much of anything."

"I'm so sorry that happened. I wish there were something I could have done. She had your love. You were good to her during those trying times."

"I helped give my mother a good life. She died too soon. I wanted to see her happier."

"I remember a promise you made to yourself. You kept it. I'm sure she appreciated that."

It was quiet as T.J. gave a little smile. It was apparent that he did what he could despite the circumstances. Ella appreciated her son and the endurance he experienced. It was harder for him to realize that he was a good son. He wanted to do more.

"I have two or three hours. Do you want to walk with me?"

"Where to?"

"Doesn't matter. There is just so much I want to know."

She wanted to kiss him as he held her hand in his. He touched her cheek. He was being nostalgic, going back in time when her face was younger, and it was her caring words that made that love stay with him.

"I can't believe it's you I'm walking with. I wanted you to be here. I hoped for it," she whispered.

"As I sat here, I pictured you up there with me in that tree when we were young," T.J. said.

"Me too. It was the first time I held a boy's hand."

"I was nervous."

"So was I."

He drew closer to her. The scene was set for them. They belonged there together. He wasn't just some stranger to her. He was what she knew was good for her heart. They walked around the park catching up on where they had been in their lives.

"Do you like your adopted parents?"

"It was hard to adjust to at first. Jane is not what I'm used to."

"What do you mean?"

"She's cold, distant, disconnected from the rest of the family. Derek, my dad, is trying to deal with her being gone. We don't know when she will return."

"So, you like your dad?"

"He's very supportive. He cares about me. I can't wait for you to meet them. Jocelyn will be home in a few months."

"We both went through losses in our lives, that's evident. I no longer have parents. I'm glad that you have them. I hope someday, they can make me part of their family. They really are blessed to have you, Cara."

"It wasn't easy when Jane made me do things that were not who I am, piano and riding lessons. Although, I do like riding after I got good at it."

"Oh, that's right, you have horses. What about piano? Are you good at playing?

"Yes. I have played in recitals and mastered many classical pieces. Jane may have had good intentions and I just didn't see it. As an adult, it wasn't so bad."

"How many horses do you have?"

"Six. My dad hired a handler to take care of them while he's out of town and when I have to focus on school."

"Just one person to take care of six horses. That's a job."

"We have other stable workers who work in shifts, but Jaime likes to be at the ranch full time."

"I thought about getting out of the city. Maybe, moving back here. I worked so hard to get to the top in this company. Moving back home means starting over."

"I know that's a big step."

"It isn't as big when I think about how much I'll miss you when I go home."

"We'll see each other again. You can call me anytime. It's funny, we are back together, and we have to be apart again."

"Let's use this time we have to give what we have to each other. I don't want to rush going home. I don't want to go," T.J. regretted.

"I know. I'm so happy I came to the park. Now I have a new memory."

"I never want to forget this day. This is forever."

After a few hours it was time to walk him to his car. He turned to look at her before he got inside. His thumb touching her cheek.

"I want you to know that today you saved me just like you did when we met. I wish I could kiss you, but I want there to be more trust between us. I would not want you to feel rushed by my feelings."

"I don't need anything else to complete me."

"I'll let you know when I can see you again."

He embraced her tightly, hoping he wouldn't let go. It was obvious by her eyes that she longed to go with him. Cara knew the distance between them would not be easy. What she never expected turned out to be so beautiful. T.J. could break free from the pain of his childhood...because of Cara.

Chapter 7

Please Come Back To Me

Derek kept trying to contact Jane. He was still in love with the woman he married. She hadn't been herself for a while. They were the first for each other. Neither of them was married before. Derek found himself working more hours and needed to get away often to hide from the pain. After selling some of his businesses and properties, he thought it would be a good time to re-find the love of his life.

Jane Dobbs was not originally the glamour queen she turned out to be before she met her husband. She fell in love with the elegant night life filled with champagne and parties. Derek was one of many donors at the event where he met Jane. She was a tall brunette with an eye for style. She went from raising money for groups in rec halls to arranging online charity invitations. She earned her income by doing photo shoots and appearing on television shows. She used credit cards to afford her wardrobe which looked like something out of a magazine.

Derek attended events when he was invited. His friend asked him to come along for an opportunity to meet others related to his business. Looking across the room, he noticed Jane. She was stunning and playing the part of outgoing hostess.

"Isn't that the girl I've seen on TV?" he asked his friend.

"Jane?"

"Yes, her. She is prettier in person. Introduce me, would you?"

"Okay, but she is way out of your league."

She smiled when introduced and invited him to sit down. He kept it casual and tried not to be too forward. They soon went outside to talk where it was less noisy. Without realizing it, they found themselves engaged in conversation for over two hours. It was getting late, close to two in the morning. He walked her to her car and after that, he couldn't stop thinking about her. Jane fell hard for Derek too. They became inseparable, spending time walking on the beach, going to dinner, and dancing together late into the night.

During sunset, overlooking the beach on a balcony, Derek asked Jane to marry him. In a few months that followed, they married in a small ceremony on the sand. Barefoot, they both wore white for their photo shoot.

Jane always wanted to raise horses. Derek got a good deal on a horse ranch in Bonsall, California. She took riding lessons and collaborated with horse trainers who professionally competed in shows. Jane was hooked. She grew to love horses more than anything.

Derek wanted to start a family and Jane refused the thought. If she became a mother, she would no longer be able to do the things she had been dreaming of. Unexpectedly she found herself pregnant. She resented her husband but accepted her daughter, Jocelyn May Saunders. Derek was very happy as a father. He loved his daughter very much and it showed. All Jane could think of was getting Jocelyn into equestrian training. It was grueling for a young girl to spend hours training at such a young age. Jocelyn wanted to be a child; Jane wanted her to be a winner. Derek noticed that Jocelyn became quiet and unhappy. He thought he would spend a day with her and take pictures of his daughter at the park. Jocelyn loved the camera. Her father handed her his camera and would let her take pictures of different objects. She was talented and her photographs turned out amazingly professional. Composition was natural to her. After Derek bought her a camera of her own, she started a book she made using her photos. Before she graduated from high school, she had photographed her horses, her high school yearbook, and started her own business taking portraits of families and their children. Photography was the one thing that made her happy. Derek was impressed by his daughter's hidden talent. Jane would not support or accept Jocelyn's choice as a career path. Her husband continually encouraged her to get to know her daughter better. Jane worked Jocelyn too much and it was taking a toll on her childhood. This daughter wanted a mother, not a boss. Jane did share some endearing times after Jocelyn won competitions. They celebrated together and there were happy cheers from Jane. But she started to change after her grandmother, the only family she knew, died in the house she grew up in. When Jane went to the funeral, she looked upon the modest house she came from. It was a life she would never return to. Her security was with Derek and her projects. Why couldn't she love her daughter? What made Jane feel cold and belligerent? Thinking about why Jane changed, Derek began to have hope when he finally contacted his wife by phone.

"Hello, Derek."

"Jane. I'm so glad to hear your voice. I called over and over. How are you?"

"I'm fine."

"When are you coming home?"

"Monday. I have an event to go to on Thursday."

"Is that the only reason you are coming home?"

"Derek, I feel lost."

"Lost? Why would you feel that way? I give you all my love. I know your background. I know life was hard for you. Whatever happened in your past has carried over into our life. I never cared about how you were raised even though you were hard to understand. I love you, only you. Do you still love me?"

"Yes, but I have so much going on in my head. I feel unfocused."

"What do you mean?"

"I want to work so I don't have to think. I don't know how to love Jocelyn."

"I think you know how. Why do you put yourself down?"

"I wasn't a good mother to Jocelyn or Cara. They must hate me."

"No, they don't hate you. Do you remember how many times Jocelyn fought with you? You had to learn to be a mother and that scared you. Teenagers need extra love and someone to hold them when they feel alone."

"Cara was in the same situation as I was. It was too familiar."

"She is fine now. She is doing what makes her happy. I spoke to Jocelyn, and she will be visiting soon. There were things you did that made me sad. I wanted to understand but felt you were acting harshly. What you did to our children wasn't right. Jocelyn cried watching her favorite horse get taken away."

"I thought I was doing what was best for her."

"You have a chance to build back what you lost. Cara is still at home. Try to talk to her. You are no longer the victim. You are the woman I married, and I am not going anywhere. I want my wife back."

"I can try."

Derek wanted to tell Cara the news that Jane was returning. Cara walked in after riding Kindred.

"Dad, are you home?"

"In here, Cara."

"I have some studying to do. I'll be in my room."

"Cara, can we talk?"

"Sure."

"I talked to Jane today."

"After many attempts, how did that go?"

"She's coming home Monday."

"I'm glad. I want to be her friend. It seems like she doesn't feel the same. Why is she so brash?"

"She has a backstory. Not that this was an excuse for her behavior, but in short, she grew up a lot like you."

"Like me?"

"Yes. She didn't know her parents either. She did not have the best life. She worked hard to make a success of herself."

"But why can't she be happy? Why can't she love Jocelyn? She wants her mother to love her. I want her to love me."

"All we can do is believe she will try."

"I will never stop trying. I want to believe someday we will be close. I'd better get back to work. Thanks, Dad."

"Love you, Cara."

She smiled as she left the room.

Derek found a package at the door from Jocelyn. She had sent some of the pictures of her travels. Her book was being edited and she was excited to share the first shots with her family. It did his heart good to see his daughter doing what she loved.

Monday arrived and Jane was finally home. She changed into her riding clothes excited to see her horses.

"It feels good to have you back, Love," Derek said.

"It's good to see you. I did miss you. Where is Cara?"

"She's at school. Did you meet the new handler?"

"I was about to go out there. I miss riding."

"I know you'll like her. Go on, go see your pretty horses."

Jane walked into the stables breathing in the familiar atmosphere. Inside an empty stall was a woman cleaning the feeder.

"Hi, I'm Jane. You must be Jaime."

"Hello. Nice to meet you."

"We appreciate what you are doing for us. I'm sorry I wasn't here to greet you."

"No need to explain. I'm happy to be here. I met your daughter, Cara. She is a great rider."

"She is. I should have been proud of her."

"I think she knows you are."

"Well, I just wanted to say, thank you."

"It's my pleasure."

Jane looked beautiful riding her horse, Pembrooke. Up high and in control was the feeling. She stopped to look at the field and then began to cry. She felt alone. She pondered on Derek's words. He was patient and kind to her even when she had her cruel moments. It was obvious that he was still in love with her. She looked around and realized she did not want to be without her family. How was she going to get Jocelyn back? She got off her horse and looked him over. She ran her hand down his back and touched his mane. Her hair was also blowing in the wind. Tears of loneliness were streaming down her face. She felt like she broke someone's heart, everyone's heart. If they were patient, she would come back to where they started from. Climbing back on Pembrooke, she trotted back.

She noticed Cara's car in the driveway. Coming into the house, Jane took off her gloves and immediately went to Cara's room. The door was partly open.

"Cara, it's Jane."

"Hello. Welcome home."

"Thanks. Are you busy? I thought maybe we can talk."

Cara did not answer. Jane led her to the sunroom to be where it was quiet. There were many windows that displayed their view. Jane had tea brought to them.

"What is on your mind?" Cara finally asked.

"I don't think we got off to a very good start when you came here."

"I wanted to. It's been many years of distance between us."

"I know. I wasn't ready to be a mom again. I didn't feel prepared to have that job. I would rather work than care for children."

"Can I ask why?"

"The truth is, Cara, I grew up feeling angry and sad. I never knew my mother. I don't even know if she is alive. When Derek learned of your story, I was hesitant. It was too close to home for me."

"We all have some backstory. That never stopped me from showing love to you."

"I understand that. I was raised by my grandmother who I called Mom. She was amazing. She died two years ago, and I was too busy to visit her before she passed. I just feel so guilty. I can't even be a good daughter."

"I'm sorry. Like you, I don't even know if my mother is alive. I've been to so many foster homes, I just accepted I would never find her."

"Cara, I'm sorry I was unkind to you. You didn't deserve that."

"Jocelyn needs you too."

"It might be too late for that."

"Why would you say that? That's your daughter, the woman who worked just as hard as you did to get to where she is today."

"Is she happy?"

"She is. She's having her photos published. That is huge for her. Don't give up on being there for her."

"Will she ever forgive me?"

"I believe she will."

"Would you like to go riding with me tomorrow, just us?"

"I would love that."

This was what Cara waited for. She had a mother, finally. Jane began to take an interest in what Cara loved. When shown her art, she admired it and wanted to display it in some of the local galleries. When she heard Jane laugh, it made her heart soar. Jane needed to be loved and feel important and useful. Patiently, this family waited on the woman with a cold heart blossom into someone Derek recognized. The picture was clear in his mind. He saw the woman he lived for; the woman who felt broken. Jane knew she would have to pick up the pieces of her life and start over. Forgiveness was in this family and so was love.

Chapter 8

This Time With You, Saved My Life

T.J. was anticipating his visit with Cara. She was flying to San Francisco to be with him for the weekend. He waited at the airport, watching for her flight arrival. There in the distance, he had seen her. Her hair in a ponytail wearing jeans and a T-shirt, she dropped her bag and ran into his arms. He held her with his eyes closed, taking in every squeeze and slowly touching her skin. He looked into her eyes, finding it hard to believe that she was the woman he was meant to be with. She found herself smiling, grinning ear to ear as she put her fingers into his hair.

"You dropped your bag. Let's go get it," he said smiling.

"Who cares? I'm just so happy to be here, right now with you."

"Nothing makes me happier," he breathed.

T.J. grabbed her bag and showed her to his car. Inside, he took her hand.

"I never realized how beautiful your hands are," he complimented.

"Oh, thank you. An architect needs hands and a brain."

"That sounds so romantic."

"No, it doesn't," she laughed.

"No, really. I think your talented and beautiful."

"Okay, charmer, where are we going?"

"I thought we would go down by the pier."

"I'd like that. It reminds me of those times I played at the beach back home."

There was a cool breeze along the pier. Neither seemed to notice.

"Are you in love?" Cara asked.

"What do you think?"

"I think so. Is it possible to fall in love given our circumstances? I think I've loved you since we were fourteen. Is that weird?"

"Not really. Think about what we meant to each other back then. I made it through the hardest times thinking about you."

"I was afraid of being brokenhearted, it was too good to be true."

"And here we are. It was meant to be and it's true."

"What were those years like when Jackson was around?"

"Hard for a kid. It was difficult seeing my mom devastated by the mistake she made. She always said she was sorry for making a bad choice. I never thought what she did was wrong. She was lonely and he fooled her."

"Did he take all of her money?"

"Not all of it. She had a separate account in her name. It was small, but he never knew about it. When he left, he took most of the furniture and walked out leaving the house a mess."

"He never contacted your mother?"

"No. But his lawyer did when he filed for divorce. He wanted to make her suffer, but the judge saw right through that."

"Did she live happy after she moved back to San Diego?"

"She did. Living in that small apartment made her feel safe. I started working for this company I'm with today and it took care of the bills. We had each other and that was all I wanted for her. When she was diagnosed as terminal, I just spiraled into depression. She never cared about being first. She loved me. There were so many times I wanted to tell you about her illness, but I felt I had to be there for her as long as I could and kept it to myself."

"You said if you didn't write, there was a good reason. I hung on to that to give me hope you would come back to me. I couldn't imagine what my life would be like knowing I'd never see you again."

He turned to her, moving the hair away from her face as the wind blew in from the bay. She was quietly looking at his face.

"What are you thinking right now, Cara?"

"How much I want to kiss you."

"Do you love me?"

"I do. I love you, Bryan Dawson."

Putting his hands on her face, he brought her to his lips. She was his comfort and joy. Her love was deep and the bond two fourteen year old kids started was rare and priceless. Their first kiss was all he imagined it would be. Soft and tender with warmth and especially, true love.

"Are you hungry?" T.J. asked.

"Yes. You pick the place."

"I love Crab Louie and some chowder."

"What's a Crab Louie?" she laughed.

"It's a fancy way of saying crab salad. Makes it more fun."

Sitting in the restaurant, the waiter brought them water with lemon wedges. Cara opened up her napkin and placed it on her lap.

"I love that you have good table manners," he said.

"Well, it's not that so much. I am clumsy when it comes to mealtime. I spill on myself, especially if I wear white."

"Good to know. I'll bring extra napkins next time we go on a date."

His comment made her chuckle.

"So, your adopted mom came back. Everything's better so far?"

"Yeah, so far. We went riding together for fun, which is a first. After all the years I spent trying to get her to like me, I'm happy she came around."

"How is Jocelyn?"

"I told her about Jane. She still doesn't have any faith that her mother will come around."

"She's fortunate to have you as her sister."

"I'm glad to have her. I'm happy to see Jane is talking more to Derek."

"When is Jocelyn coming home?"

"Soon. Her schedule is crazy. We want to celebrate her new photography book when it comes out. I'm sure it's going to be a hit."

They ordered their food and engaged in small talk.

"Do you have any other family besides your mom?" Cara asked.

"My dad's mother and I were close. She was the one who gave me that pocketknife. I still have it. She died from heart disease just like Dad."

"T.J., we are a family now; you always have been. I know many people wouldn't understand that, but we are that close."

"It seems like yesterday when we first met."

"I did climb that tree before I saw you."

"Really? I hope you weren't wearing heels."

"No. I was missing you and I wanted to see our names again. I saw that you carved B.D. by my name."

"Yes, I did. I was hoping to see you come around the corner again and we could start over."

"I had the same dream. Being without my mother has been hard, but you helped fill that void. Marcia told me that a family can be anyone who loves you, an aunt, a grandparent, anyone."

"That's true. I think even though they are not your real family, they can be."

They left the restaurant to walk the wharf. Letters, phone calls, nor FaceTime would never top the day Cara and T.J. were together face to face. After their meal, she wanted to know something. Cara grabbed his arm and asked, "T.J., what is love to you? What does it mean to you?"

"Well, I think love goes deeper than anything physical or material. The day we met; I was getting very little sleep from what I heard at night. I'd cry and I couldn't focus on school. I saw you at times in the park and I thought you were pretty. I wanted to climb as high as I could to take away the fear I was going through. Then I saw you get closer to the tree, and you looked even more beautiful than I thought. So many things were going through my mind. 'I could love her', I thought. So, what love means to me is the feeling I had when sadness left me that day when I saw your face. It was genuine and honest."

"Genuine and honest. That was a good answer. This is why I trusted you when we met again. I knew you were still the same as back then. I was never best friends with a boy before. It was different and new. You saved me too."

"Some people may think we're crazy. Who falls in love at fourteen? I did. Cara, there is nothing that will stop me from feeling the way I do about you. You were abandoned, feeling alone without your mother and look at yourself. You are full of so much talent and life, it amazes me."

"I know inside I looked like I was fine, but I cried from loneliness, too. As I grew up, I couldn't believe someone would want me. Then all I thought of was you."

He stopped walking and turned to face her.

"Look, it doesn't matter whether we've had years of history, or we met yesterday. I love you. I do. My mother taught me how to love someone. I could have had a lot of girls after I moved away. But for some reason I knew in my heart I'd find you. I give you my word, Cara. I will always be in love with you. I don't want you to be afraid that I would leave you."

"I have faith in you. I know we are human. I know even with the best intentions, lovers get hurt. You are still the one for me."

They talked about what staying together meant for them. Cara hoped that T.J. would love her no matter what they went through. She held that promise close to her.

It was time for Cara to go home after three days together. Saying goodbye wasn't always easy. She grew to hate the word. A kiss and an endearing look sent her on her way. T.J.'s heart was aching. He couldn't wait to meet her family. Sitting in the airport watching her leave, he took out a picture of Ella. He wished she were alive to see that her son made it and found the woman who gave him the strength to carry on through the worst times. Ella was a gentle woman and no matter what they went through together, she would have been proud of her son.

Chapter 9

Welcome Home

The time finally arrived for Jocelyn to come home. She had been away for eight months and had a month before returning to her next assignment in Ireland and Spain. Derek was planning to have a catered party of fifty guests. Jane was nervous recalling how things went before Jocelyn left.

The backyard was well lit. Lanterns gave a glow to the spaces where some guests already gathered. An array of dishes was spread on several tables decorated with fresh flowers and champagne flutes. There was a classical band playing soft music in the background. It was a casual event, no suits or gowns. Derek was tired of going to events dressed up and this time he wanted to feel relaxed. Before the guests arrived, Derek went to find Jane.

"Darling, are you almost ready?"

Jane was sitting in front of her vanity mirror.

"Derek, I..."

"Jane, what's wrong?"

"It's going to be hard seeing Jocelyn again. I'm not sure she will even want to talk to me."

"I think what you need to focus on is that she is coming home; to us. We are celebrating as a family. What happened doesn't matter tonight."

"I want to learn to love her."

"You will. You already have found it in your heart to love her. Believe in forgiveness."

More guests arrived. The sunset was nearing the horizon painting orange and pink in the sky. Jaime was putting the horses into their stables as dusk set in. She looked over at the festivities and pondered what it would be like to be there. She was invited but chose not to attend. Her business was about being there for Derek and the job she had to do. With dirt on her hands and wearing her cowboy hat, she retreated to her truck for the night. She would return in the morning.

"Derek where is the guest of honor?" a man asked.

"I had a car sent for her. She should be here soon."

Cara was getting ready. She couldn't wait to spend time with her sister and tell her the news about T.J. She knew Jane and Jocelyn would have a tough time seeing each other. She believed things in time would eventually work out for the best. Her family was healing and that was all that counted for Cara.

Jocelyn came into the house and went straight for Cara's room.

"Hey there!" Jocelyn cried out.

"Joss! Oh, my goodness. You look so good! Dad's having a party in your honor so get ready. Not formal, but casual so wear something cute."

"Wow, you look amazing. You got that look."

"What look?"

"The look of love. I want to hear all about it. I know you've been dying to tell me."

"Yes, I have been. Now, go get yourself ready. Go by and see your mom. She's in her room."

Jocelyn was hesitant but she admitted to herself that she missed her mother. She quietly knocked on the door and heard, "Come in."

"Hi, Mom."

"Jocelyn, my dear. I'm so happy to see you."

She hugged her close.

"I'm so glad to be home."

"I hope we can start fresh where we left off."

"Sure, we can talk later."

"Your father loves parties but tonight I won't be wearing my finest."

"I know you'll look nice even if it's not fancy. I better get ready now."

She turned to leave the room.

"Jocelyn."

"Yes."

"Welcome home."

"Thanks, Mom."

Jocelyn thought that was as good a start as any. Jane was different but in what way? She may have realized what she had; a good family that loved her.

Derek was coming into the house when he saw his girl. She ran into his arms.

"Dad!"

"Jocelyn! You look beautiful. I'm such a proud father."

"Dad, I missed you. You didn't have to do all this."

"Everyone loves your new book. Honey, the pictures you took are spectacular. Ever since you were young, I knew you would make it. You have the gift."

"Well, I did have help. I had such a great crew. It was tiring traveling so much, so tonight is a big relief."

"Did you see your mother?"

"Yes. I don't want to talk about issues tonight. We will talk soon. I'm happy she's home."

"Me too. Come on, Cara is greeting the guests."

Everyone was out enjoying the party for Jocelyn. Jane made her appearance shortly after the festivities started.

"Doesn't Jocelyn look beautiful?" Derek asked.

"Yes, she does. I see you invited the same old gang from the country club," Jane said with a bit of sarcasm.

"Well, they're you're friends too. Let's try to have a good time."

"Very well. I'll start by having a glass of champagne."

Jocelyn was sitting with Cara taking about her travels. Then she brought up a conversation about Jane.

"I love Dad for doing this for me, but everyone seems so old."

"That's just because they are his friends. So, how are you feeling talking to your mother?" Cara asked.

"Okay so far. What happened while I was gone and why did she come back?" Jocelyn inquired.

"I don't really know. Your dad didn't go into detail about it. He did tell me something about your mom I never knew."

"What's that?"

"Their family situation was a lot like mine."

"I knew that. I know she was close to her grandmother. What I know about my mom is that she has always wanted to be in control. She fired some of the best trainers that we became close to. She was forceful and unkind. I'm not so sure she has changed how she thinks."

"Are you going to give her a chance?"

"I can hear her out, but I'm still not convinced."

The sisters were watching couples dancing to the music.

"You mentioned that you met someone. I need the whole story," Jocelyn said very intrigued.

"Well, it's a long story but I can give you the short version."

She proceeded to tell Jocelyn about how she reconnected with T.J. again at the tree at Lindley Park.

"Cara, that's amazing. What are the odds you would see him again?"

"He's been hurt. I know he still has sadness from the abuse and loss even if it has been years since he has seen Jackson."

"When do we get to meet him?"

"Soon. He'll come before you leave."

"Take me to that tree someday, okay?"

"Sure. I'd love to take you there. You can put your name on it by mine."

Derek approached his daughters and held his hand out.

"I would like a dance with my daughter, Jocelyn. Cara, you're next."

Cara watched her father and sister dance together. It was beautiful and she wished T.J. were here to share this with her family.

"Are you enjoying the party?" Jane asked.

"Yes. It's elegant but simple."

"Derek never liked elaborate parties. I like dress up and meet new people. That's me, I'm the party person. Of course, he invites the same old people. That gets tiring," Jane said uncomfortably.

"Jocelyn is having a good time. Are you happy to have her home?"

"She's my daughter. Of course, I'm happy she's home."

"I wasn't trying to pry into your feelings. I was..."

"It almost feels like you are judging me."

Cara had to say something, tired of Jane's uncomfortable response.

"Jane, I have been your adopted daughter for ten years. Derek has shown me so much respect. I can't call you mom because I can't have a real relationship with you. I wasn't judging you. I was giving you a chance. I feel sorry for Jocelyn. Excuse me."

Cara left the party. Derek saw her upset and followed her. Cara was crying in her room.

"Cara, it's Dad. What happened?"

"She says things that are not true.. I want her to accept me as her daughter, but she fights it. If she only knew how much I want this for us. She doesn't even try."

"It is tough trying to see things her way or what she's feeling. I know she can be up and down at times. I'm sorry she hurt you."

"I want more from her than just love. I want her to be my family."

"I think you and your sister should have a day with her. Maybe, go riding and connect with each other."

"I don't think it will help."

"All we can do is hope for the best. Jane can be a giving person. She is just so afraid of failure. Admitting she has a problem with Jocelyn is hard for her. She wants to be praised for her success. When she feels threatened, she gets defensive. I'll work on trying to get her to be kinder to you."

"You don't have to do that."

"I do because I love you. She is going to go riding with you and Jocelyn, end of discussion."

He smiled at her and kissed her cheek. Cara rejoined the party. Derek approach Jane.

"How are you tonight?"

"Why does everyone keep asking me questions? I'm fine."

"Good, because tomorrow I want you to take the girls riding with you."

"Why? I don't think..."

"It doesn't matter what you think. They are hurt by you, and you need to talk with your daughters."

"Daughters?"

"Yes, daughters. Cara is our family too. You know this. Listen and try to understand them. Even if you don't want to, you are going to ride with them. I hope I made myself clear. I love you, but this distance between you and them has got to end."

"Fine. I'll do it."

"Good answer. See things from their eyes. Don't think about yourself. They love you; I know they do."

"Okay, Derek. You made your point perfectly clear!"

"And Jane? There is no excuse why you can't show kindness." He left her presence.

After the guests went home, the caterers and cleaning crew worked on packing up. Derek let the girls know Jane agreed to ride with them. Both were accepting the idea.

Jocelyn came into Cara's room.

"Hey, how are you after the party?"

"I'm okay. Do you think Jane really wants to go with us?"

"I don't know. It's hard to tell with her."

"I know it will be good for us to talk things out."

"Probably. Don't be so sure she will be agreeable to anything I want."

"I wish T.J. were here."

"You miss him?"

"Yes. I feel different being in love."

"I've never been in love. Does it feel strange that you hardly know him?"

"No. I had a good feeling about him when we were young. When you know, you just know."

"I would like to know how that feels. My parents do all they can to try and stay together. My dad works even harder to please Mom. He has such an unselfish heart."

"He and I really like each other. He is a good father and I think despite what Jane is going through, he makes being here a happy place."

"That's Dad."

They said goodnight and went to bed. Cara couldn't stop thinking about how much she wanted her mother to accept her. She had to believe what her dad said. Hopefully soon, Jane would change the way she loved her daughters and her husband.

Jane was quiet as she was getting ready for bed. She climbed into bed beside Derek.

He quietly said, "Goodnight. I love you, Jane."

She replied, "I know. Goodnight."

As he turned out the light, he pondered on how much longer it would be before Jane humbled herself to earn trust and show love. She seemed to love her horses more than her daughters. Derek never wanted to press for information as to why Jane felt lost or a failure. He had faith it would work out and she would return to him the way she was when they first fell in love. Jane had changes she needed to make. What would it take to get her to see how showing love to her girls would make a difference in their lives? Could Jane make that move and give up her selfish ways? Does she want to be loved?

Chapter 10

The Pain Will Go Away

Jaime had arrived early to start her day. Holding her coffee in her hand, she came into the barn to greet the stock. She treated them as though they were her own. Her voice was always anticipated by the horses. She was hoping to ride after her chores.

"Well, hi there, Jaime. You're here early," Derek greeted her.

"I have those days where I just get up early and want to be here. Jane can sure pick good breeds. I love these horses. Pembrooke is my favorite."

"He's a good boy. Jane and the girls are going riding today. After they return, you can brush them. They'll need a rest."

"Good idea. I thought I'd go for a ride this morning if that's okay with you."

"Absolutely. Get out there and have a peaceful morning."

"Thanks."

Jaime loved to pet each of the horses on their nose before she started her day. The sound of their whinnies were like music to her. She loved the smell of the fields after a good rain. The aroma blew through the arena. The stables were always clean, thanks to her. Her farrier skills helped care for the animals she loved so much. Getting dusty and dirty at the end of the day was her pay. She wasn't afraid of hard work and loved what she did for Derek and his family. She sat on a bale of alfalfa as she sipped her coffee. Looking out toward the large opening of the barn, she reflected on how she still lived alone and came home to no one at the end of each day. She didn't mind living that way, she learned to prefer it. It was something she had to accept when it came time to move on from a past too painful to recall. She became secure with her pattern of life. Being around animals gave her a sense of pride knowing she was responsible for taking care of something. They were beautiful, fit, and she enjoyed the job. The years she spent on this earth made her feel worthy of something.

Jane was in her dressing closet putting her riding clothes on. She expected the girls to ask her questions and she didn't want to feel attacked. In her mind, she always doubted herself. She didn't want someone else to add to that commotion in her mind. It was hard for her to confront what she knew she needed to do to make things right. Others couldn't see it, but she felt incapable. As she looked at herself in the mirror, she saw the woman she always wanted to be, but wished for more. She tried to make horses her main career, but she was too involved in her endeavors. Jane had to face her fears and she had to be there for her daughters.

Jaime brought out the horses for their morning ride.

"Are we ready?" Cara asked.

"Guess so," said Jocelyn. She whispered to Cara, *"This feels more like a therapy session than a ride."*

"Just give it a chance."

Their property was about forty acres. There were many trails on and off the property to ride and some wooded areas that were not developed but trimmed out for hiking. The women rode toward the woods on the trail that had a small pond nearby.

"Your father asked me to have a conversation with you both."

"I think we can be calm about this," Cara said.

"This feels awkward, but I have to ask. What do you expect from me, you know, the daughter you raised? Why are your expectations so high?" Jocelyn was pressing for a good answer.

"Do you have to be so direct?" asked Cara.

"We're grown women. Let her answer the question," Jocelyn replied.

"I have more experience. Getting you involved in the arts was a way for you to see where hard work will take you. How many kids hate music lessons but when they become good at it, they are glad they endured the lessons? If they quit, they regret it. Pushing you would help you to do well in other aspects of life."

"That's what you believe? Okay, I understand the regret, but if I never did the things you asked me to do, I still would have turned out fine. I needed you to believe in me without pushing me into something I disliked."

There was sarcasm in her tone. Jane tried to hear what her daughter was explaining. It required her to be genuine and kind with her words.

"Let me ask you something. Do you like riding?" Jane asked.

"Yes, I do but..."

"So, you like riding and you learned how to ride properly. I know you hated it at first, but you learned something. There are families out there who are not as privileged as you are. I think you should have appreciated what I did for you."

Jocelyn stopped and got off her horse. "You did this for you! You did so many things to hurt me. You sold my horse, you told me you never wanted to have children, and you didn't even welcome Cara into our family. All you stirred up was conflict. You never even made an effort to say, I love you to me or to Cara."

"Do you want me to lie about how I felt? I wasn't ready to have a family!"

"Why? Is it because you never had one yourself? You only thought of yourself, and it suited you. For once please, think about others. Think about what it would mean to me. Show how much you love me!"

Cara was quiet. This was between them to work out. Afterward she spoke.

"I think what Jane is trying to say is she wants you to appreciate that she was thinking of what was best for us."

"Yeah, I heard what she said," Jocelyn said frustrated.

"I agreed to talk with you hoping this would make sense for you. Nothing I say or do will be good enough for you. I tried to make an effort and you didn't. I think we're done here." Jane was overwhelmed.

Jocelyn wasn't thinking about how disrespectful she sounded. Cara understood what Jane was saying but Jocelyn was caught up in her deep emotions.

"That's it? Aren't you going to think about what it will take to fix us?" Jocelyn said trying not to cry.

"I heard every word. I can't be here anymore. I wanted this to be an opportunity for us to connect, but you are defensive about my answers to you. I was trying to understand and now I'm uncomfortable."

Jane took off hard on her horse without her daughters. She was crying, upset that her daughter may have had a justified reason for her feelings, but Jane was right too. Jane felt like she had failed and there was nothing she could do at this time to mend her relationship with Jocelyn. There may have been hope, yet she felt her pain was too intense to think clearly. Suddenly, her horse tripped his hoof into a shallow hole. Jane was thrown forward injuring her shoulder and hitting her head. She was unconscious. Her daughters caught up to her and saw her lying on the ground with a bleeding scalp. She was still breathing.

"Mom, can you hear me?"

There was no response.

"Cara, go get help! I'll stay with her."

Cara was an excellent rider. She bolted out as fast as she could to reach the barn. Jaime had medical training in first aid and Cara called out to her.

"Help, Jaime, help."

"What is it?" Where's Jane and Jocelyn?"

"Jane fell off her horse and she's bleeding. Jocelyn stayed with her. Come help!"

Jaime grabbed the first aid kit from her truck. They both rode together. As they approached the scene, they could see she was sitting up but still in shock.

"Jane, can you walk?" Jaime asked.

"No. I can't move my arm."

"I'm going to call 911. She should go to the hospital," Jaime said. She managed to put a bandage on Jane's forehead.

Cara called on her cell phone and the paramedics arrived, putting Jane in the ambulance. The girls were holding on to each other as they watched their mother leave. They called their father, but he didn't answer.

Guilt overtook Jocelyn. "Why did we fight? It's my fault. I upset her." She was trembling with panic.

"She'll be okay. We can't stress about it. Please don't torture yourself with it. She's alive, it was an accident," Cara reassured.

"How is her horse, Jaime?" asked Jocelyn.

"He'll be swollen for a few days. I'll have the equine vet check him out. No broken bone that I can see. I'm not sure we should walk him back though. I'll get the horse trailer and some liniment. Wait here and keep him calm."

"I need to call Dad again."

"Take a moment to breathe. Call him when we get back to the house," Cara said.

Jaime loaded the horse, and the girls walked their horses home. They called the vet to come out and Xray the horse's leg. Jocelyn reached Derek and related Jane's accident. He left work for the hospital.

"I'm here to see my wife, Jane Saunders."

"Take a seat, I'll let the doctor know you're here."

Derek waited ten minutes. The doctor told him she had a concussion and a dislocated shoulder. She had some bruises on her face that weren't going to clear up anytime soon.

"She's going to be fine, Mr. Saunders. I'm glad it wasn't worse. She can go home soon. Follow up with her physician."

"Thank you, Doctor."

Derek's cell phone rang. It was Jocelyn.

"Dad, I want to come see Mom."

"We're on our way home. She's going to need some rest. I'll be home soon."

"Jaime said Mom's horse will be all right. He has a sprain. Is Mom okay?"

"She's going to be fine Jocelyn. Don't worry."

Derek put Jane to bed. He closed the door and let her rest. He wanted his daughters to explain what happened.

"Sit down. What caused all of this? I thought you were just going for a ride."

"We were talking about our relationship. I asked her questions and she got irritated. She got upset and rode off without us. When we found her, she was on the ground. I'm sorry, Dad. It's my fault," Jocelyn confessed.

"Why was it your fault?" Derek asked.

"I was upset at her. My questions were frustrating, and I know I came off rude."

"Why would you do that to your mother? She agreed to work things out."

"She tried, she did. All I thought about was the bad things that happened. I know she felt guilty because of me."

"Honey, getting thrown was an accident. It wasn't your fault. You could have been more respectful. If you hurt her with your words, you should apologize."

"We had a fight. I didn't want it to go that way."

"She's physically going to recover. You can talk to her when she has rested. Give her time to heal. Concussions are serious."

Cara got up to go out to the barn where Jaime was at. She needed a break from all the stress inside and she wanted Jocelyn to have some time with Derek.

"Are you okay? That was scary, but I think she's going to be fine," Jaime consoled.

"I'm fine. Thank you for helping. "

"I didn't do much. But you're welcome. I'm glad the horse is okay. Sometimes these kinds of accidents are not good news for a horse."

"Can I stay here for a while?" Cara asked.

"Sure. You want to talk?"

"You don't want to hear my troubles."

"I think I can handle it."

She put her hands together on the gate as she began.

"All my life I felt like I never fit in. I saw my share of foster homes and lost many friends. I wanted this to be my home, and it seemed impossible to get through to Jane but I know she wants to try. I should give her a chance since she did communicate with us. It is important for me to be loved by her too. I didn't agree with Jocelyn and the way she took out her frustrations on Jane. Somehow we can get through the hard stuff. I'm not sure how Jane will feel after she gets well."

"I know you have a good family here that loves you. Jane has her own insecurities to deal with. I think she loves you underneath all of that. Kind of like a burr under the saddle thing."

"Right now, I miss my real mom so much. I think about her often, whoever she is. Jane is the only mother I have. It was hard watching her, and Jocelyn have words."

"Families have their fights. It's not forever. Sometimes they work themselves out like a sliver in your finger. It might hurt for a while, but eventually, that piece of wood gets out and the healing begins."

"You talk like a rancher. I take it you have had experience with slivers in your hand."

"Yeah, in my hand and in family. Things happen and we cry, we get hurt, we move on. I've fallen off of so many horses. I couldn't afford to be afraid. I had to get back on and try not to fall again. No matter how many times I fell off, I never gave up. Don't give up on Jane. She needs you more than she realizes."

"That's what I told my friend T.J. when he wanted to run away. I told him his mother needs him when he wanted to give up."

"Who's T.J.?"

"He's a boy I knew back in San Diego. I met him at a park when I was fourteen. He was going through a tough time in his family. His mother died not too long ago. Now, he is the love I thought I would never find."

"Oh, you're in a relationship? To meet your first love when you were fourteen is rare."

"T.J. and I have supported each other because we went through some pretty big losses. I hope you get the chance to meet him too."

"I'm just a hired rancher. A cowgirl, I guess you could say."

"You're more than that to me. You are a good friend. I feel comfortable talking to you and you made me feel better. Thank you for that."

"No problem. You should scoot on home. I need to finish brushing these guys and clean up."

Cara started to leave when Jaime stopped her.

"Hey, Cara. You're okay in my book too."

Because of the loss Cara went through, her kind of pain was hard to understand. Jamie made all the difference in helping her see that there was always hope.

Waiting a day since Jane fell, Jocelyn thought this was a good time to see how she was feeling.

"Hey, Mom. How are you?"

"I feel beat up. The worst was when they put my shoulder back in."

"You look better."

"I might have some bruises, but I think my ego is the most bruised."

Jocelyn sat on the bed facing Jane.

"I thought about what you said. You were right. I would have regretted it if I never learned any of the things you ask me to do. I can't imagine never being able to ride."

"I can imagine that for me. Just a small joke."

"I get it. Cara told me Jaime fell off horses many times. You never give up and keep trying."

"You never gave up on me. I could see that. I've always had this anger built up inside me. When I met your father, I felt rescued and loved. I needed to control everything. I thought control would make everything right. It was wrong. It didn't make anything better. It pulled you away from me."

"Mom, I didn't know how to tell you how much I needed you."

"You were loud and clear. When we were riding and you told me how you felt, I was listening. I did hear what you said. It was hard to hear but I heard what was in your heart. I thought I was a failure as a parent."

"I never said you were a failure. I didn't understand what you wanted from me."

"I wasn't ready to be a mom it's true, but when I saw you for the first time, my heart loved you. I didn't want you to end up like I did when I was young and impetuous. I made a lot of mistakes. I was afraid for you to go to Europe. But it turned out okay. You published your first photography book. I took a look at it while lying in this bed. It's beautiful."

"I should have said thank you for what you tried to do for me. As I grow older, I will appreciate it even more than today."

"Jocelyn, I'm sorry for everything I've done."

"I'm sorry too. You gave me a good start. I'm an adult who learned to have goals and work hard because of you. Don't say you are a failure. Dad brought Cara to me. I was lonely and she put the light into my life again when I thought I lost you."

"You haven't lost me. Because of my selfishness, I could have lost everything and been right back where I came from."

"I don't want you to go to that place. There is a good reason Dad picked you out of all the women out there."

"Why? Why did he pick me?"

"Because you wanted to be loved. He didn't want to imagine his life without you. No matter what you've been through, he stayed, patiently waiting for you to come back." Jocelyn reached out and stroked her hand.

"Do you think Cara would forgive me?"

"She has. She is just that kind of person."

"Can you bring her in?"

"Sure."

Cara came near the door and peered in. Her hands were folded together.

"She wants to see you. Don't worry, it's all right."

Cara looked at Jane's face. Her bruises were more prominent than the day before. She looked out of place in her well-kept room.

"Hello, Cara. Come sit by me." She patted the bed.

"You look better. I was afraid when I saw you hurt."

"I'll be back on that horse after I'm healed. All these years of riding and I fall off for the first time in ages. I guess I had it coming."

"I never want to see you hurt like that again."

"Cara, I know it has been an adjustment for both of us. I was wrong. You had nothing to do with the way I treated you."

"I've missed having a mother, I've missed you. I wanted us to be close. I'm sorry it has been so hard for you. All these years have made my heart feel broken. No matter what has happened between us, you are my mother."

"I want to tell you a story. My mother was a sad person. She had me very young and I wasn't cared for properly by her. I never knew my father. My grandmother didn't want me to go to foster care like you did, so she adopted me. I never saw my mother after that. It was lonely especially when other girls would have those times with their moms. My grandmother was old, and I was made fun of when she came to school events with me."

"I would have been happy to have any family claim me. We both know what it's like to be without a mother," Cara said.

"Yes. Cara, I wasn't ready to go back to my past when you came. I made my fortune and worked hard to hide the pain I was in. Falling off that horse gave me so much to think about. I treated you like the girls from school treated me. For that I am deeply sorry."

"It's okay that we have a lot in common. I just want you to love me for who I am. Don't dwell on my past."

"Derek loved you when he saw your picture at the adoption agency. I was afraid your past would hurt you like it did me."

"With that behind us, can we love each other?"

111

"I think I can do that. I should have loved you when you needed it the most."

"Right now is perfect, Mom."

Jane reached out to touch Cara's hand. The two were no longer trapped in their past lives. Jane wanted to get back to being the mother she should have been to her daughters. There would be mistakes in a family, but love healed the stabs to a wounded heart. Cara knew things would never be perfect. Her understanding of Jane's childhood gave her the will to be present during her painful and happy times. Cara's love blanketed any flaws her family had. She was now another support for Jane's pain. No one knew how long Jane would feel that way. No one was used to her feeling positive. Jane started to realize that she would need extra support outside of her family. Soon enough, she would come to be close to the one person she never expected to be drawn to, Jaime Cooper.

Chapter 11

The Visitor

T.J. was preparing to meet Cara's family while Jocelyn was still home. He had taken some time off work to be with the woman he loved. He was on the phone with his friend Caleb, who was very close to him after Ella passed away. He was the attorney who helped T.J. with his mother's assets. Jackson wanted to take everything from the marriage. After selling the house, Ella got the equity and Jackson got half of the joint checking account they shared. Ella had a secret account for T.J. Some of the money she saved was from Thomas' life insurance and the sale of the house. Caleb became a valuable support over the years.

"Hey, man, are you going to meet Cara's family today?" Caleb asked.

"Yeah, I was just about to get out the door."

"I know how you pack. You pack more things than a woman does. How long are you going to be gone?"

"A week. Cara's sister is home and she's only there for two more weeks."

'This is a big step, meeting the family," he chuckled.

"I'm not afraid of taking big steps if that is what you mean."

"All jokes aside, I'm happy for you. You deserve to have a good life with the woman you love."

"Thanks, Cay. Hey, someone's at the door. I'll call you later."

"Okay. Have a safe trip."

T.J. moved his bags to the side as he walked to the door. Opening the door, he was shocked to see who appeared.

"Hello, Bryan."

"Jackson, what are you doing here? I thought we got rid of you after the divorce." T.J. was nervous since he wasn't expecting to see Jackson. His voice was stern when speaking to him.

"I'm hard to kill, I guess. Wow, you've done good for yourself. How did you make your fortune, with your mother's money she stole from me?"

"Leave my sight. You're not welcomed here."

"I came for what's mine. Where's Ella? I want to talk to her." He pushed on the door.

"She's not here."

"How do I know you are telling me the truth?" Jackson was forceful and unkind.

"She's not here!"

"Where is she? I demand to know where my wife is." He was pushing the door harder while T.J. held on so as to not let him in.

"She's not your concern anymore. She's not your wife. Why do you need to know where she is?"

"She was my wife!"

"Was your wife. Don't forget that. Get out!"

"She took what was mine. I gave her everything and from what I can see, you got it all."

"Leave or I'll call the police."

"You're threatening me? You sure didn't get away with that when you were a skittish little kid. I scared you straight."

"You did nothing for us. Don't come back here, don't mention my mother again. Now leave."

"Tell Ella I'll be looking for her, Bryan! You don't want to mess with me." He started to walk away then turned around to say something to him.

"You know, you are such a coward. You don't even have it in you to fight." He laughed walking down the hallway.

He walked out of the apartment complex yelling something unintelligible. Downstairs, his friend was waiting for him.

"Did you get what you wanted?" Geoff asked.

"Nah. He's hiding something. I'm determined to get what's coming to me. He knows where Ella is."

"What is your next plan?"

"Revenge! I've hated that kid ever since I first laid eyes on him. Every time he talked about Ella's dead husband, I wanted to knock him out."

"You should find out where she is."

"I'm going to find her. She was never on my side. I'm glad I divorced her. It gave me more money after we split. But I'm sure she is hiding."

"If you come back, be sure not to get caught. You do have a warrant. I don't think you want to go back to jail."

"Right now, I don't care. I'm going to call my lawyer. He's just as slick as I am. Ella's out there somewhere and I'm going to find her."

Jackson lost his job after he became angry at his boss. He depleted all of his income and lost his home and car. He was staying at Geoff's house, plotting a way to make some money. His biggest dilemma was how to get back at T.J. He admitted to his friends he never loved Ella. He was used to taking advantage of anyone who would fall for his lies. He was narcissistic and acted like a controlling parasite who ruined everything Ella and T.J. built. His failure and low self-esteem were on the hunt for the one person who stood in his way of having it all. He would never admit that he was jealous of T.J. He wanted to sue them both, claiming he didn't get enough money when they divorced. She was awarded the house but sold it to move back home. When threatened by her ex-husband, she filed a restraining order. He continued banging on her door and yelling his demands. He wanted the house and felt the judge was unfair. It was clear his intentions were not good. He was the unwelcomed dragon who used his power to control and destroy good hearted people.

T.J. fought hard for his mother right down to the end. He calmed her anxieties and guilt making her laugh during those painful times her illness took over. Watching his mother take her last breath, T.J. held her in his arms, promising he would never let anyone hurt them again. His parents were buried next to each other. It was hard for him to realize he no longer had parents. Jackson was evil and still alive. While he knew his parents, his mind was thankful they were good people to look up to. Life happened and after Ella's funeral, the light returned to him when he found Cara again.

T.J. closed the door and locked it. He informed the police that he was going out of town and didn't want Jackson coming to his home again. He didn't think he owed any explanation to Jackson about his mother. So many bad memories were coming back to his mind. Even though he knew his mother had died, she was safe. How did he even find his place? Would he return? He had to get it out of his head and concentrate on seeing Cara. This unexpected visit was not what T.J. was prepared for. He thought he would never see the creep again. What was he claiming was his? He got half the assets in their divorce. He looked at his watch and realized he needed to catch his flight. Grabbing his bags, he went downstairs from his apartment to catch the taxi to the airport. He sent Cara a text message informing her that he was leaving. His anxiety declined as he touched down at the airport. A rental car awaited him. With what happened back at his apartment, seeing her would be a welcomed sigh of relief. T.J. was approaching the home where Cara lived.

"Is he here yet?" Jocelyn asked again.

"No. he's not late."

"I know. You've been staring out the window like you're watching a pot boil."

"Is Jaime here? I want her to meet him," asked Cara.

"She will be back this afternoon. She had to help her friend move."

Cara looked back out the window and seen a car driving in. She couldn't help but go out to hold him.

"Cara, I'm finally here!" T.J. said as he got out of his car.

"How was your flight?"

"Boring. I can't wait to meet your family."

T.J. wanted to talk to Cara about the encounter he had with Jackson. He wasn't sure how she would handle it. He would wait for a better time.

"Where are your parents?" he asked.

"They are still on their Caribbean cruise. I want you to meet our horse handler, Jaime. She'll be here later."

"Great."

"Oh, this is my sister, Jocelyn."

"It's nice to meet you."

"You were right Cara, he's cute."

117

"Are you trying to embarrass me?"

"I hope so. C'mon, let's get you settled."

T.J. looked around at their beautiful home. He had never seen anything so luxurious. There was a spare room near Derek's office where T.J. put his luggage. It had its own private bathroom. To him it was like being in a hotel suite.

"So, what would you like to do first?" Cara asked.

"For right now, I'd like a glass of iced tea and a chair in your backyard. I'd love to talk with you."

"That sounds amazing. I'll get it." Cara disappeared around the corner.

T.J. and Jocelyn went to get comfortable in the backyard.

"My sister is very happy she met you, T.J."

"I'm happy too."

"Cara is a brave person. She's been through a lot in her life. From what she tells me, so have you."

"Yes. We both miss our moms. She's really made my world a better place. I'm going to meet your parents, right? Will they be back home before I leave?"

"They left yesterday. I'm not sure when they'll be back. They know you're here."

"I don't want to miss my visit with them. Cara talks about Derek all the time."

"Yeah, he's a great dad. Well, I have to make some calls to my friends. I have so much to catch up on before I leave."

"It was good to see you, Jocelyn."

Cara came out with two glasses of tea.

"Sorry it took so long. The ice maker got stuck."

"That's okay. I like your sister. She's nice."

"She is. We go riding together and spend time talking about you."

"Oh, really? I hope it's all good things."

"It is."

"I'm glad to be here. I wanted to talk to you about something that happened before I got here. I was thinking about how this news would make you feel."

"What is it?"

"As I was getting ready to leave, Jackson came to my apartment."

"Jackson? What did he want? Did he hurt you?"

"No. He was rude and sarcastic as usual. He said he was looking for my mother."

"Did you tell him she died?"

"No. He doesn't need to know that."

"How did it make you feel when he showed up?"

"I have to say, a little bit scary. He is always so forceful with his words. He claims he scared me straight. He is so crazy."

"Do you think he'll show up again?"

"I don't know. I think he wants money. That's all he ever wanted."

"I want you to be safe."

"I'll be all right. If he comes again, I'll call the police. But right now, I'm here to talk about us. I love where you live."

"Oh, you like our place? We have forty acres."

"Forty acres? Plenty of room to ride horses. Any other animals?"

"Just critters and birds. That's what Jaime says."

"Will she be here soon?"

"I think so. She's a gifted horse handler. She and I have become good friends. She's older and experienced in so many things. When my mom had her accident, she stayed calm and knew exactly what to do. She keeps a first aid kit in her truck. It was a good thing she came prepared."

"That's great. Does she live on the property?"

"No. She gets here early in the morning, just when the sun peeks out. She has a way with these horses, probably all horses."

"How is your mom since her fall?"

"She's better. Her and my dad had to take this trip. We are all getting along better, and I can finally call her Mom."

"How does that make you feel?"

"Good. I could never call Marcia 'Mom' because I never knew when I would leave. It would have been too painful for me. Jane and I have a new understanding because I found out that she was abandoned when she was young like I was."

T.J. smiled and reached over to give her a kiss. They looked out at the horizon, observing wind-swept clouds hovering above the field. It felt peaceful and safe.

"Are you going to take me riding while I'm here?"

"Of course. I want you to meet my horse, Kindred. He is the gentlest horse."

"Interesting name."

"I named him that because he is my family."

"That's important to you, isn't it?"

"You know it is. We can go over to the stables if you'd like."

He set his empty glass down, "I'd like that."

With his arm around Cara, the two of them walked over to meet the other part of her family.

Jaime had arrived shortly after T.J. did. She was sitting on Pembrooke when Cara called out to her. Dressed in her chaps and hat, Cara could see her in the sunlight near the barn.

"Jaime, wait! Over here!"

"Cara, who's with you?"

Jaime slid off the horse.

"This is T.J. He's here from San Francisco. I told you about him."

"Hi, T.J. So nice to meet you."

"A pleasure. You look the part. I like your outfit."

"I get pretty dirty wrangling horses, feeding and cleaning up after them. The joy of my life."

"How is my mom's horse?" Cara asked.

"Much better. I'm taking him out for a slow walk later, he's watching for potholes."

"Yeah, I heard he had a bad fall. I'm glad he's better," T.J. said.

"Would you two like to ride with me?"

"I've never ridden a horse before," T.J. said.

Cara nodded, "Well, you can sit behind me on my horse. Right behind my saddle. It will be fun."

"Okay, let's try it," T.J. agreed

Cara went to saddle up her horse. T.J. watched her use her skills to get the horse ready.

"Wow, you're a real professional," he said.

"No, Jaime's the pro."

She looked back at Cara with a smile.

"All our saddles were fit for us. Each one fits the rider so that we're comfortable."

"I like that you know that." He was very impressed.

They turned their mounts in the direction of the easier trails. They went slow taking T.J. into consideration. He was still a little nervous.

"Are you okay?" Jaime asked.

"Yes. No trotting, okay?" T.J. said a bit nervous.

"You got it, nice and slow," Jaime reminded.

Jaime wanted to get to know T.J. better since Cara always talked about him as a part of her family. She was impressed with how respectful and kind he was.

"How long are you here for, T.J.?" she asked.

"A week. I haven't been out much since Mom died and seeing Cara gave me the drive to just take off. I needed to see this family of hers."

"Derek is a truly kind man. You'll like him."

"Jane is nice too," Cara added quickly.

"Yes, she is," Jaime said.

"This is so nice and beautiful here. I really miss Southern Cali. My mother moved south of here after her divorce."

"Cara said you had a mean stepfather."

"Yes. He showed up at my home before I left."

"He knew where you lived? Do you feel safe?" Jaime asked.

"I'm not going to worry about it. He has a big mouth, and he uses intimidation to get information out of anyone he meets to get his way. I didn't tell him much, just to leave. I moved in with my mom for a while after he left. We needed money so I moved back to San Francisco and got a respectable job. I traveled back and forth a lot to make sure she was okay. I stayed with her until her last breath. I don't know how he got my address."

"Stay safe. He doesn't sound too friendly."

"He's not. Thank you for that."

They talked about each other's lives. T.J. talked about how many times he carved his name in the trunk at Lindley. She was fascinated at how he mentioned the tree and Cara saving his life with support. Jaime got to know the man who came out of a complicated family situation.

T.J. unexpectedly asked, "So, Jaime, where is your family? Do you have any children?"

She paused and didn't answer for a while. Feeling hesitant to reveal too much about her life, she finally found the words.

"No, don't have any children. Most of my family is gone."

"Oh, I'm sorry to hear that."

She wanted to change the subject. There was a side of Jaime she didn't want anyone to know.

"I think we should be heading back. I still have a few chores before sunset."

"Okay, Jaime," Cara agreed.

T.J. whispered to Cara, "*Did I say something wrong?*"

"*I don't think so.*"

They returned to the stables. Jaime got off her horse first.

"Nice to meet you, T.J.," Jaime said as she put the horses away.

"Same here."

"Jaime is very handy and helpful. She has a private side, too. I hope you enjoyed riding with us."

"I did. Thank you. I still feel like I'm sitting on a horse though, a little sore," he rubbed his pants.

They had dinner together talking about the silly thing's teenagers did when they were young. Cara talked about how she loved the makeup and styles when she was younger and she would never wear again. T.J. mentioned how his voice changed and how long his hair was. They talked about love, crushes, and how Cara got into Architecture.

"This has been fun getting to know you better. I don't think I have ever talked this much," T.J. admitted.

"I love hearing you talk. You have a soothing voice."

"How's school? How much more time do you have before you graduate?"

"I have about two years left. I have been working with my dad on some projects and I get to intern for some other designers to gain more experience. It's mostly for education. Dad is working on a new two-story library now. I am learning a lot from that job."

"Two years? That's a lot of book learning."

"I love it, though. I am halfway through. Buildings are a real art. The shapes, the sizes, and designs, it's all composition."

"I'm sure you will be amazing at it."

"Thanks."

"I just love being here. When Jackson came to my apartment, I thought about getting away permanently and moving here to be near you."

"Can you get a good job here?"

"Not as good as the one I have now. I would have to give up everything to be with you. I would be willing to do that."

"I can't ask you to do that."

"I miss you. These times that we spend together are like little treasures I want to save. I want to someday go to Lindley Park with our own children. I want a life with you, not the most successful job out there. Your love will always be there. A job can always change."

"My favorite thing about being in love are the memories. You know I want to have more of those with you."

"So, what do you think, do you want me to move back here?"

She jumped in his arms.

"Yes, yes. I do!"

He kissed her. His fingers slid behind her ear. The embrace was Cara's way of sealing that love and commitment. When they breathed again, he looked into her eyes.

"I want our children to have your eyes," he whispered.

"I want them to have your smile," she said as they both laughed.

She could see forever with him. He was willing to give up anything to be with her. He wanted to make her happy. They were apart as children, as adults, and they received a new chance at life together. Cara never feared they would be apart again.

Jocelyn received a call from Derek saying they would be home in time to meet T.J. before he left. They expected to arrive the next afternoon. It was also getting close to the day Jocelyn would be leaving for Ireland. Cara saw her family growing. This family unit was going to be stronger than ever no matter what storms would come.

Jaime was sitting in the stable thinking about how much she wished she had a family. T.J. did nothing wrong asking her that question. When she felt lonely, it was the company of the horses that kept her feeling she had some purpose. She sat inside her truck and broke down emotionally, crying. Inside the home where Cara lived, were members of a family that had love and closeness. For Jaime, this was just a dream, a dream that she could only wish for. What else was there? What hope was there in the heart of the lonely horse handler, Jaime Cooper?

Derek and Jane loved meeting and visiting with T.J. after returning from their trip. It was nice to be surrounded by family. T.J. never had the privilege of a big family. His distressing thought were diminishing the more time he spent with the Saunders. It made his decision clear, he needed to leave San Francisco.

T.J. had to catch the morning flight. He would be looking for a new job in San Diego. Cara knew he would be back. The waiting would be hard, but she would have what she longed for. "I will never forget you," is what they both said when they were younger. He touched her cheek and tenderly looked at her. She didn't believe in goodbyes. T.J. may have taught her how to patiently wait for good things to come. He would return.

Chapter 12

For Cara Jo

In San Francisco, T.J. was having a lunch meeting with Caleb about protecting his mother's name and account. Jackson had not reappeared but the thought of what he was capable of made him anxious. There was a lot on his mind, from his job change and missing Cara, to Jackson's threat. Many times T.J. woke up in the middle of the night with nightmares of his childhood. He was scatter brained in his mind thinking of the harm Jackson could do to his life. Something good had to come to him and he had to believe he would get justice.

"How have you been? You look beat up," Caleb inquired.

"I've been exhausted looking for a job in San Diego. It's tough out there. There are mostly entry levels to apply for. I haven't had much sleep. Sometimes I think he's watching me each time I leave my home."

"Don't do that to yourself. I'm working on what we can do to keep him away from you. I can't get an address where he's living now. Let me do my job. Just relax."

"All I can think about is how much I want to change my life for Cara."

"She must be worth it to go through this much trouble."

"She's more than worth it. Each time I see her, I draw closer to her, and I want to be where she is."

"Is it the money that's hard to transition?"

"No, it's not the money. Money was all Jackson thought about when he was with my mother. I want to be able to take care of Cara. Give her the support she needs."

"She sounds like a reasonable woman. I'm sure she will be happy as long as you two are together, right?"

"Yes. There are a few job offers I could apply for. My credentials are off the charts, so I shouldn't get any rejections."

"There you go, keep up that positive attitude."

"I still don't know what I'm going to do about Jackson."

"Do you feel he's dangerous?"

"He sure rattled my cage when he was here."

"I can see what he can do to get a restraining order on this guy."

"Thanks, but I think it will be okay."

"I'm here for you if you need anything. I gotta go. I have to be in court in less than an hour. Take care of yourself."

"Yeah, thanks."

T.J. was the kind of man who needed support when he felt things were too much for his mind to handle. His mother always had a warm way of calming him down. Cara had that gentle side of her that cared about his feelings. He was supposed to be a man, a responsible man, but fears from childhood often broke him down and overpowered him. He wasn't sure if Jackson would return or if his threats were going to resurface. He had to focus on taking care of his love, a woman who never asked for much except to be loved.

Jocelyn was getting ready to leave for the airport. Jane clearly observed her daughter was becoming a success. All the years that she tried to hold her daughters back were such a waste of time. They were strong, confident women who had the drive to go for what they felt was best for them. Jane was no longer feeling like a failure, but a mother who was watching her fledglings fly on their own.

With her bags in the trunk, Jocelyn stood in front of her mother.

"Jocelyn, while you were here, I saw how much you have grown. You are so gifted and I'm glad it wasn't too late for us."

"Thank you. I have my mother back."

"Call soon, Joss. I love you," Derek said as he pulled his daughter into his arms."

"Cara, I'll miss you too. I want to hear more about T.J. Can't wait until we all get together soon."

"Love you sis. Have a good trip."

Jocelyn sadly drove away thinking how she would only be able to visit with her family through phone calls and FaceTime. It would never be the same as those weeks she spent at home, drawing closer to those she loved.

After driving away, Cara noticed Jaime near the barn with some rope over her shoulder. She walked over to talk to her.

"Hey, Jaime. What are you doing here today? Dad gave you the day off."

"I thought I would organize some things in the barn. This rope was tangled so I fixed it to hang on the hook."

"Are you okay today?"

"I'm fine. I saw Jocelyn leave. We're all going to miss her."

"You should have come to say goodbye."

"No, that's your family. I don't want to impose."

"Jaime, you've been with us a while. Anyone I get close to, I call family."

"You, you love me like family?"

"Well, yeah. And I love your passion, the love you have for these horses, and the devotion you have for all of us."

"Your dad said I can come here anytime I wanted to, to ride Pembrooke. I came here to do a job for Derek. I never expected to be loved by any of you."

"You don't have to shy away from us. You've done so much for me. I love your wisdom and kindness. I wish I knew more about you."

"What good would that do? I don't have much of a life."

"Why is that? Why are you alone?"

"I guess I chose it that way. It keeps me safe."

"Do you feel like you are not safe because you've been hurt?"

Jaime put the rope on the hook and walked over to touch Pembrooke. Cara watched her expression as Jaime turned back to look at her.

"Cara, sometimes we make mistakes and how we heal from those mistakes is not very easy. I keep to myself because it's easier to just deal with me and my personal issues. We all have them."

"What kind of issues could you have? You always make me wish I could be more like you."

"That's a nice compliment but you have your whole life ahead of you. I've learned to love where I'm at. I'm okay, really."

"Jaime, how old were you when you started working with horses?"

"About twenty one. I rented a room in a house with an elderly woman who didn't want to give her horses away. She couldn't care for them, so she asked me to live on her ranch and help out." She rubbed the horses' neck. "From there I started working with veterinarians and handlers. I wasn't the type to get dirty or shovel horse manure but over time, I learned to like it. It became who I am today."

"I know you want a family. I see you looking over at our place when we have people over to visit. I worry you aren't happy with your life."

"We don't need to talk about this anymore. I'm fine with the way my life is. Everyone gets a little lonely. As long as I the horses and being able to come here, I'm happy. Don't you worry about me."

"You're a good person, Jaime."

"Thanks."

Cara wanted to understand more. This tough woman was more than a hired hand. Cara felt something was holding Jaime back from telling her about a possible troubled past. It could be that Jaime was born a loner and nothing was wrong. Or was something painfully hiding deep inside this lonely woman who needed love? Whatever the reason, Cara could see that Jaime wasn't completely happy. She loved caring for horses, but why? She was at the ranch early every day and would go home each day to no one. Cara wasn't convinced Jaime was fine.

Chapter 13

The Prince Conquered The Dragon

T.J. finally was hired by another marketing company after months of trying to find the perfect job. They were impressed by his resume and experience. The job wasn't full time yet, but he didn't mind as long as he could be closer to Cara. He was going to keep his apartment until the job was ready to start, the following month.

Caleb did some background checks on Jackson Perry to see if there was anything on his record that would help keep him away. He had a friend who was a police officer who became familiar with Jackson's record of crimes.

"What did you find, Paul?" asked Caleb.

"This guy has done some serious time. He has a warrant for violating a restraining order and traffic tickets. He's been arrested many times and has been involved in domestic violence with a weapon. He's not someone to mess with."

"What can we do? T.J. is not sure if he will be back."

"He may not return. Call us if he comes back. He could be potentially dangerous."

"Paul, I've been staying at his house so he would feel safer. Do we have something to worry about?"

"I think for now, you're safe. I know you want to help but try not to handle him yourselves."

Caleb was concerned. Jackson's history did not look promising. What he hoped was that T.J. would move out before anything happened.

Jackson had been driving by the apartment. He and Geoff were planning to face T.J. They would watch to see who was going out and coming into his place of residence. The day before, Jackson and Geoff assaulted a store clerk. They were wearing hats and sunglasses to hide themselves from the cameras. Jackson's lifestyle was brutal and soon enough, it was going to catch up with him. He was an angry man, a man with a past that left him with nowhere to turn to but a life of crime. T.J. always felt upset that such a man would fool his mother and take everything she owned. Ella never cared about the material possessions she lost. She knew it was more important to be released from the painful bondage that she was under. She gained strength and power to unchain her emotions. She was no longer trapped. T.J. made it possible to rescue his mother and shelter her from harm. This he did well. He protected her money, spoke to attorneys and never revealed to Jackson that his mother died. His loyalty was proof that he would do the same for Cara. He would love her, protect her and fight for her no matter the cost.

Cara was excited to hear that T.J. would be moving soon. She had been cramming in some extra study time to be ready. She kept herself busy talking to different architects and designers hoping to do an internship with some prestigious companies. She was tired and noticed that her eyes were straining from the stress of long study nights. For a few months, her eyes had been bothering her. Jane thought she would check in with Cara since the light was on in her room.

"You're up late. It's 11:30. Are you going to finish soon?"

"Yes, I'm trying to make up for some homework that is due. I got distracted."

"T.J.? I get it. Okay, lights out in five minutes."

"Okay. Goodnight."

Cara rubbed her eyes and stretched as she finished the last paragraph. She needed to keep up her studies and try not to think of T.J. when she needed to focus. She slept well.

In the morning after arriving to the ranch, Jaime was caring for one of the mares showing signs of birthing. She had been in labor and called the vet to come check Bailey out.

"Well, what's the diagnosis?"

"She's going to deliver soon. You got a new one on the way." The vet knew Jaime could do this on her own. He left giving her the confidence that it would be fine.

Jaime gave Bailey a pat on her neck and said, "You're going to be a mommy!"

Cara walked over to the barn seeing two people inside.

"What's going on?" she asked.

"Bailey is going to have her first foal."

"That's good news."

"I want you to help me with the delivery."

"Me? I don't know anything about horses giving birth."

"You don't have to know much. Come here and feel her belly."

Cara walked over to give a gentle touch to the mare as she laid down to labor.

"It won't be long. I'm glad you're here to experience this."

"Me too."

A few hours passed and the new foal was on its way out into the world.

"Cara, can you see the legs?"

"Yes. She's working so hard."

"She knows what to do."

After a few pushes, the new foal was born. Cara gave Bailey a rub as the new mother cleaned it off.

"It's a male foal. What should we name him?" Jaime asked.

"Dash? He looks like he could be a fast and competitive horse."

"Okay, Dash it is."

"Bailey is a good mother. Thank you for letting me be a part of this."

"I wanted you here. This is why I love what I do."

"I want to be a mom someday."

"I think you would make a good mother."

"That's a wish I hope comes true. I've always pictured scenarios in my mind of what it would be like. I want T.J. to be with me in that thought."

"He loves you very much. I think things will go your way."

Cara blinked and rubbed her eyes. She frequently did that throughout her day.

"Are you alright? You look tired," Jaime asked.

"Oh, I've been studying a lot trying to catch up on some homework. T.J.'s visit got me behind. For a moment I didn't want to do any studying. Crazy, huh?" Cara looked down.

"Love makes us do crazy things."

"It sure does."

"Derek said T.J. is moving back this way. That's got to be exciting for you."

"He can't move yet. He has some things to finish before he can get here."

"It sounds like you two are in for the long haul. Do you ever think about marriage?"

"Yes, I never mention it because I don't want him to feel rushed. I can see myself married to him." She paused and looked at Jaime. "I just have to ask and if you don't want to, you don't have to answer."

"What would you like to ask me?"

"Have you ever been married?"

Jaime turned to walk a few steps to think about her question.

"Yes. I was married for a very short time."

"I'm sorry. We're you divorced?"

"No, he died. A drunk driver hit him as he was coming home from work."

Jaime looked down. She didn't want to imagine reliving what happened to her man.

"Oh, Jaime. That must have been a painful time for you."

"It was a long time ago. We were high school sweethearts. Anyway, I should finish breaking the hay for feeding time. Bailey is going to need her nourishment for her new baby."

"Okay. If you need to talk, fetch me anytime, please."

Cara felt the pain Jaime must have experienced. She had no idea that she was once married and in love. Knowing this gave Cara a new perspective. She was already fond of her. Now it was easier to sense why she put so much time into her work. Cara thought she would go to her room and get back to her schoolwork.

T.J had a meeting with his current supervisor. He had received notice the week before that he was quitting to relocate to San Diego.

"Bryan, it won't be the same without you."

"Thanks, Steve. I've been here three years."

"Whatever you do in your life, you'll go far. We really liked having you here. And if we ever open a firm down there, we will look you up." He shook his hand firmly, "Take good care."

"Thank you."

T.J. had less than a week left before he started his new job. He gave Caleb a call letting him know he was on his way home. Cara decided to call T.J as he walked in the door of his home.

"Hi there. Are you counting the days?"

"Of course. I wish I could leave now. I found an apartment in Oceanside. It's near the beach so I can pick you up for those walks on the shore."

"You better promise that. I hate going to the beach alone."

"You will never have to do that."

"I can't wait. Right now, I have so much homework."

"I know what it feels like to play catch up. Don't tire yourself out too much."

"My parents tell me I go to bed too late. I have so much work, though."

"I know. Pace yourself. You'll get it turned in on time."

"I gotta go. I'll talk to you later," Cara said.

"Okay. Rest, please."

"I will."

"Who was that?" Caleb asked.

"Cara. My visit with her got her behind on her studies. I feel guilty."

"Hey, don't feel bad. You enjoyed yourself. What's for dinner?"

"How about some take out?"

"I'm down. Pizza or Chinese?"

"Pizza. I'll call in for a pizza delivery."

"Great."

T.J. was answering some emails waiting for the pizza to arrive. Caleb was watching T.V. They heard a pound at the door.

"When did you order that?" Caleb asked.

"Ten minutes ago."

"Someone's at the door already."

"Caleb, get away from the door," T.J. whispered loudly.

Caleb went into his bedroom to get ready to call the police when T.J. opened the door a few inches.

"I warned you! I'll bet you didn't think I would come back!" With an unexpected burst of energy Jackson pushed his way into the apartment. The force knocked T.J. to the floor. Geoff was waiting outside with the car running.

"Who do you think you are barging into my home?"

"I just found out from my lawyer that Ella is dead. Why didn't you tell me? You loser!" Jackson grabbed his collar and pulled him halfway up demanding an answer.

"She is gone and no longer your business. Get out!"

Caleb was listening and called Paul to send the police over right away. He was torn between staying quietly out of the way and rushing to protect his friend.

"I'm going to get what is mine. You got most of my money and I should have had that coming to me!" He dropped T.J. back onto the floor.

T.J. stood up, quietly and slowly said, "You get nothing because you are nothing."

At that moment, Jackson landed a closed fist into his face knocking him down. He was bleeding from his lip. Jackson then picked him up and repeatedly hit him. T.J. brought his arms together to block the blows. He felt weak and thought for a moment of all that he and his mother went through while he was in their home. Did that make him feel weak? This is the guy who instilled fear into him when he was a child. T.J. reminded himself that he was a child no longer and a little bigger and heavier than his aggressor.

"Had enough? You always were a coward. I think your mother knew that about you."

"You will never have control over me. You are not a real man."

"You have a lot of guts to talk to me that way and now you're going to pay!"

T.J. could feel his adrenaline building up. He felt the power in his body growing. He was ready to end the torture. Jackson got ready for another swing, thinking he was going to finish him when T.J. released a hard left to his ribs then a right to the head. Jackson fell down, unconscious. T.J. stumbled over to Caleb to talk to him.

"I called Paul. The police are on their way. Oh, T.J., he messed you up bad!"

"Hand me a towel. I'll be alright." He was holding his ribs.

Caleb couldn't believe what happened.

"Dude, is he dead?"

"Nah, I finally got tired and ended it. Besides, he was the one who said he was hard to kill. I got some closure now. He won't bother me again without paying for it. You're going to jail, Jackson!"

Just then Paul and two officers came in and picked up Jackson. They arrested him as he was coming out of his blackout. Paul came over check on T.J.'s wounds.

"I need to get a report on what happened. Caleb told me most of what went on."

"I guess I defended myself."

"This guy has a bad record. I'm sure he will be spending a lot of time in jail. I'd think about filing a restraining order to keep him away from you in case he gets out."

"T.J., let's get you to the hospital just to check you out," Caleb advised.

"We'll get you back on your feet. Let me help you walk."

"Hey, thanks Cay."

"No worries."

"Did someone order a pizza?" asked the delivery guy at the door.

Paul took the pizza and put it in the kitchen.

"We're eating this later."

They left the hospital. T.J. had a few broken ribs and some contusions. He felt very sore and just wanted to end this day with some rest.

"What a night, huh?" Caleb asked.

"That's an understatement. I feel like I slayed the dragon."

"You did. You got rid of what tried to control you. I'm sorry it happened this way."

"I've wanted to lay him out since I met him. With him in jail, I feel like I can start my life with Cara. I'm going to ask her to marry me."

"Taking the vows. You deserve it."

"I'm glad you were here. Thanks man, for calling the police."

"I won't lie, that was scary. What a psycho." Caleb was a little shook up.

"He was more than that. He thought he could ruin my life. I didn't realize that he had so much power over me. Now, that part is over."

Caleb decided to move in with T.J. They went through so much together and Caleb wouldn't leave his side. It was like he saved his life. He did.

Convicted of numerous crimes, Jackson Perry would never hold power over T.J. No one would be allowed to break his spirit. He had it in him to fight the battle he was dealing with. His mother would never see his conquest, but he defeated the nightmare and put it to rest. Bryan Dawson was a victor.

Chapter 14

The Journey Begins

Cara heard about the encounter, and she was worried for T.J. He assured her that he was safe and was on his way to see her. Driving in, he had Caleb with him. Cara ran out of the house into his arms.

"Careful, I'm still recovering from these broken ribs."

"Oh, I'm sorry. Your face looks so bad. Are you sure you're okay?"

"I'm good. Don't fret over me. I'm just happy to be here with you."

"Hi, I'm Caleb, T.J.'s friend."

"Best friend too. He saved me. He and I are going to be roommates," complimented T.J.

"Welcome, Caleb."

They sat around the outdoor fire together. Cara held onto T.J.'s hand and then she suddenly stood up to walk away leaving the conversation. He followed.

"Cara, what's wrong?"

"T.J., you could have died. I don't know what I would do if he..."

"Hey, hey, it's okay. I'm here and alive. Jackson cannot go near me anymore. They locked him up. We're safe."

He held her while she cried.

"I never want to be without you ever again."

"You won't be. Where's Jaime?"

"She's just about to leave. She's in the barn."

"I'm going to get her and bring her here to be with us."

"We've asked her many times to join us, and she always says no."

"I can be convincing."

T.J. walked into the barn looking.

"Jaime! You in here?"

"Over here. I heard about the altercation. You okay? I hope you make a good recovery."

"Thanks. Hey, why don't you come join us?"

"Oh, no, thank you. My shift is over, and I need to get home."

"Why do you need to go home? You know you don't have to be so tough, Jaime. This family loves you like one of their own."

"I know. I don't want to disrupt the occasion."

"Jaime, I want you to know that I need you beside me tonight."

Jaime took a breath, not expecting to hear that.

He put his hand on her shoulder, "Please, Jaime. You do so much for this family. I need you to be part of this." He opened his hand to show her why. She saw a small box in his hand.

She thought about it for a few seconds.

"Well, what do you say?" T.J. asked again.

"Okay, I'll come."

T.J. walked with her. He put his arm around hers and tousled her hat while laughing.

Walking into the back yard, Cara saw Jaime walking with T.J. She was surprised he got her to come over.

"How did you get her to come over?"

"I told you, I'm convincing."

The family was gathered around. Derek got Jocelyn on FaceTime to be there and then he got everyone's attention.

'Thank you for coming, everyone. Tonight, we are celebrating. We are so glad that T.J. is safe and on his way to a full recovery. We are happy to have Jaime with us, and we have a special guest via the Internet.

"Hello, everyone!" shouted Jocelyn.

"Joss, what a surprise!" Cara shouted.

"Cara, I am here for your big night."

"My big night? What are you talking about?"

"Honey, we are all here for you. I gave my blessing. Go ahead, T.J."

"Cara, there is nothing in this world that would have convinced me to turn away when we were kids. The tree at Lindley Park kept me safe, your face made me feel secure and unafraid to love. Tonight, I give my heart to you, here on bended knee."

Cara had her hands over her mouth. Happy tears streamed down her face in rivulets as she looked down at him.

"Cara Jo Sanderson, will you be my wife? Marry me and complete my life with your love and devotion." He opened his hand to reveal a small engagement ring.

Jaime watched Cara become the happiest she had ever been. She recalled her own marriage and how she missed her husband who died many years ago.

"Yes, T.J., I'll marry you."

"Girl, you're engaged!" said Jocelyn as everyone clapped and gave the happy couple hugs and best wishes.

"I know you are going to be happy, Cara. I love you," said Jane.

Derek was happy to see his family all together for the engagement. They celebrated with champagne and dined together. A special cake was brought out to share with all their loved ones. Jaime started to turn and leave when Cara stopped her.

"Jaime, you're not leaving, are you?"

"I am. Cara, I'm happy for you. It's hard for me to be here and enjoy myself."

"I know you're missing your husband. I am glad you were here for me and T.J."

"I've been in your place. It was a memorable time for me once upon a time."

"Will you be here for the wedding?"

"I'll try to make it."

"Promise me you'll come."

"Okay, I promise."

"Goodnight, Cara."

Jocelyn wanted to talk to her sister alone. While the festivities were still going on, Cara took the tablet into her room.

"Cara, I want to tell you something. I don't want anyone to know, yet."

"A secret? What is it?"

"I met someone while I was in Ireland. He's a photographer, a good friend of one of our set designers."

"Jocelyn, that's great news."

"He's going to be moving to the States when I get done with this tour. I'm going to come home to get a job there locally. I'll still be in photography. I can't wait to get back home now that you're engaged. I want to be with my family again."

"You actually got to live your dream since you were a kid. I guess we're growing up."

"I guess so. You're going to be a great wife. I can't wait to help you plan your wedding."

"Now that is going to be fun. We get to shop!"

"I love you, Cara."

"Love you too. I can't wait for you to come home so we can meet, what's his name?"

"It's Patrick Flynn."

"With a name like that, we gotta meet him. He sounds like a swashbuckling hero."

"Maybe he is," Jocelyn laughed.

The sisters could see their lives changing. They were getting older and settling down was in their hearts. They wanted a family of their own, children, and gatherings every year.

Cara said goodbye to Jocelyn since overseas hours were late. As she stood up, something was wrong with her vision. She couldn't see well. Everything looked blurry. She blinked and rubbed her eyes. Her vision was going in and out with blurs of light. She made her way downstairs and talked to Derek about it.

"How long have you been having issues with your eyes?"

"About a year. I never thought it was a problem. Just too much time at the books. Lately, it has been worsening. Dad, what could be wrong? I'm worried."

"We'll take care of it, dear. We'll find out what is wrong."

They made an appointment to see the eye doctor the next day. Cara didn't want to worry about it any longer. She thought that she might need glasses, or she was working too hard. Whatever the reason, Cara would find out soon enough what was wrong.

Chapter 15

Loved At First Sight

Derek and Jane accompanied Cara to their Optometrist. T.J. wanted to be there but needed to be at an orientation meeting. They ran all their tests and examined her thoroughly.

"How long have you been having trouble with your eyes?" the doctor asked.

"A year. I thought it was because I was tired. I have been studying a lot and I wasn't getting enough sleep."

"Did you tell your parents about it when you noticed it?"

"No. I didn't see it as a big deal. It would go away then it would come back. Do I need glasses?"

"Cara, you will need glasses, but it will be only temporary."

"So, that's good, just temporary."

"No, it's not good. You have a disease called vision impairment."

"What does that mean?"

"You're going blind. There isn't anything we can do to stop it from happening."

Derek interjected, "There has to be a surgery, right?"

"It's degenerative. I'm sorry, Cara. We can give you some glasses to help, but the reality is, you will lose your total vision. We just can't say when."

"I want a second opinion," Cara said sternly.

Cara sat stoically but she was crying.

"I can give you the number of a good Ophthalmologist. He is the best at treating these kinds of eye disorders. You're welcome to give him a call."

"Doctor, what should we do in the meantime?" asked Jane. "It feels hopeless."

"Don't feel sorry for me." pleaded Cara.

"Cara, please." Derek voiced concern for his daughter.

"What, Dad? I still have a life to live. I have to finish school, get married, see the sunset every night, see my sister. If it's all going away, how am I supposed to feel? Tell me, what am I supposed to feel?"

"I don't know what to tell you, Cara. We hate this news too," Derek said as he tried to be understanding.

"Here's Doctor Russell. Call him if you need to. I'll leave you alone for a moment."

"Cara, the truth is, you are going to need help."

"I can see fine right now. Maybe, the doctor is wrong."

"We can call Doctor Russell. Then you would have your answer. Do you want to call him?"

"I don't know what I want to do. I need to get out of here."

Derek and Jane didn't know what was in store for their daughter. They knew they were going to have to eventually help Cara as her blindness progressed. Cara was devastated, feeling like the news crushed her whole future life.

Cara came home and went straight to her room. She wanted to talk to T.J. He would understand.

"Hi, Cara. What's wrong?" He could hear her crying.

"T.J. I just came back from the eye doctor. Remember when I was telling you about those times I had trouble seeing, like I strained my eyes?"

"Yes. What did they say?"

"He told me that I am gradually going blind and it's not reversible. It's permanent. I don't know when I will be fully blind. I wasn't expecting such unwelcomed news."

"Oh, Cara. I'm sorry about this. How are your eyes now?"

"I have times when I can see well and then its blurry. It lasts for a while then it goes away. Lately it's been getting worse."

"Listen, this doesn't change anything about our life together."

"Yes, it does! I can't get my Architecture degree; I won't be able to see all the things that make me feel alive. Everything is going to change."

"I will still love you."

"That's not going to fix it."

"Cara, my vows to you are promises that no matter what we go through together, I will stay by you."

"I don't want you helping me do everything! I'm capable of doing things on my own."

"Okay, you made your point. We can cross that when we get there. But my advice is that you slowly prepare yourself for what is coming."

"I don't want to."

"I know."

"I don't want to talk anymore. I'm sorry."

Cara hung up the phone. It was a lot to take in. She was young and ready to plan her wedding. Now there was a roadblock ahead. This was the biggest challenge she ever had to face. Derek let Jocelyn know about Cara's condition. She begged to return to be with her, but Derek asked her to finish her work because Cara was fine for the moment.

Cara did see Doctor Russell the next week and he confirmed what she did not want to hear. Now that she received her second opinion, Cara just wanted to be left alone with her thoughts on how she was going to deal with this.

She was curled up on the couch in the family room.

"Hey, there. Do you want some company?" Derek asked.

"No, but you can stay."

"Why are you here alone? Shouldn't you be with T.J. or planning your wedding? You still have your sight."

"Yeah, but for how long?"

"Why care how long? You still need to enjoy the moments. Right now, you have the opportunity to use what vision you have left. Feeling sorry for yourself isn't going to make it easier."

"I'm not feeling..." she sighed

"Cara. You're here alone, all you do is mope. Life throws us curves. None of us know where it will take us. Unexpected occurrences befall all. Seize the day. It's all so cliché but it's true in your case."

"I'm afraid. What am I going to do when it goes dark?"

"We help each other as a family. And face it, you are going to need some help. Jane wants to help with the wedding plans. Let's start living."

"I wish Jocelyn was here."

"You're wish is granted," said Derek looking at the door.

"What?! Joss! What are you doing here?"

"We got done early. I'm home for good."

"Come on, we have a wedding to plan!"

"Where's Patrick?"

"I knew there was someone I was forgetting. Patrick, this is my sister, Cara."

"Nice to meet you."

"You too. Jocelyn, he's adorable."

"Yep, he is."

Cara remembered the words of her father. She had to use what time she had left to plan the wedding she dreamed of. Cara wanted a wedding at home. They planned out the catering, the cake, the dress, the décor, and the invitations so all the ones they loved could attend. Jane could have hired a wedding coordinator, but she wanted to do this for her daughter. The wedding was still months away and there was still so much to do.

Jocelyn drove Cara to Jaime's house to invite her to the wedding. She lived in a small cottage she renovated years ago. She didn't have her own horses because she liked taking care of others before herself. She owned an old pickup truck. Her place had two bedrooms with the guest bedroom stacked with books on horses and medical veterinarian manuals. There was tack and a few saddles in the room. There were pictures of different animals that she photographed. This was the first time Cara had been to Jaime's home.

"Park over there, Jocelyn."

"Cara, have you ever been here before?"

"No. I really want to talk with her about coming to the wedding. She promised me she would."

"Then why are we here?"

"I want to see where she lives. I need to talk to her."

"She's not expecting us, so I'll wait here in the car."

"Suit yourself. I won't be long."

Cara walked through the dusty walkway to the door. She knocked on the screen door and saw Jaime coming.

"Cara? What are you doing here? Is everything all right?"

"Yes. I wanted to give you an invitation to the wedding. May I come in?"

"I wasn't prepared for company so excuse my clutter. Sure, come in."

"It's fine. It looks like a cowgirl lives here."

"What's on your mind?"

"I just found out that I am going blind. I don't know when it will happen, but lately, it has been more difficult to see."

"I'm sorry to hear that news. Did they tell you what is causing the blindness?"

"They just said vision impairment. They think my retinas are detaching. I don't know why, but there is nothing the doctors can do at this point."

"Cara, I didn't know. Why are you here to tell me that?"

"Because I trust you. I want to be a close friend to you before my sight gives out. You have given me full support and right now, I need that. I have never been to your home. I'm sorry if I imposed, but I had to be here. You take care of everyone and yet, you seem so alone. I want to be part of your life, Jaime."

"Cara, I just don't get too attached to the people I meet. There's good reason for that."

"You only need a small circle of friends. You will always have us."

"Cara, I have other things I need to do today. I wasn't expecting anyone to be here. I know you care about me, but I need to handle things my way."

Cara saw a picture on the mantle. She walked over to you to get a closer look. Holding it in her hand, she looked carefully at it.

"Is that a picture of you and your husband?"

"Yes." Jaime was not comfortable answering.

"I thought you said you never had children. You're holding a baby."

"I don't have children anymore. Cara, I'm sorry, you'll have to excuse me. I need you to leave. We can talk tomorrow."

Cara saw she was frustrating Jaime. She turned to leave.

"I apologize for staying too long."

As she was walking out, she glanced at pieces of mail sitting on the table with other bills. Jaime could do nothing but stand there as Cara picked up the mail to look closer. Jaime was nervous and wringing her hands hoping Cara would just leave.

"What is this? Jaime, why does your name read Jaime Sanderson? What's going on?"

"Cara, I..."

"Who are you? Why do you have my last name on your mail? I thought your last name was Cooper." Cara was disturbed by what she had seen. Her thoughts began to race.

"Cooper was my mother's maiden name. My married name is Sanderson."

"What does that mean? Why are you..."

"Cara, there were so many times I wanted to tell you. I wanted you to get to know me better before I told you."

"Before you told me what? What are you trying to say?" Cara's voice was quivering as she began to cry.

"I am your birth mother. You are my daughter."

"What? No, no you're not, that can't be true!"

"I didn't want you to find out this way. I wanted to tell you so many times, but I was afraid."

"Afraid? You secretly kept this from me while you were at my parents' home. What could you be afraid of?" Cara's voice got louder.

"I didn't want you to be angry."

"How did you know Derek?"

She turned away to look at the picture again. "He's my cousin."

"So, Derek is my family? There was family out there and no one claimed me? What kind of people are you?"

"Cara, please understand. Let me explain it to you."

"I want to know everything! Tell me how this all went down. I want to hear your pathetic reason for doing this to me!"

"Okay, try to be calm and listen. I was married when I was nineteen. Matthew and I were best friends since high school. A few months later after I was married, I was pregnant. When you were born, Matthew died. I was alone with no money, and no place to go. Derek was living out of the country. I had postpartum depression and I missed my husband. I never told Derek I left you at the hospital until much later. I wanted you to have a good life. I couldn't care for you. He adopted you after searching for you. I wanted to meet you, get to know you, but I was too afraid. I came to work with his horses and be closer to you. I was out of my mind back then, panicked I would lose you if I didn't care for you properly. I had no other way to be close to you. So, I came to work for my cousin where you would be."

"Is that me in that picture?" Cara was emotional.

"It is. That's your father."

"I feel sick just thinking about how you lied to me, you are a fraud!"

"I'm not a fraud. I wasn't ready to find you. You were well taken care of, and I felt better knowing you were happy. I didn't want to disrupt anything that was keeping you happy with a family who cared for you. Seeing you in love, growing up in my cousin's house, learning to love life, that's what I learned about you."

"I have to get out of here!"

"Please don't leave upset."

"How long were you going to keep this from me? How many more years? I'm going blind! You had many chances to claim me, but you chose not to."

"You fell in love with me, as a friend. I felt it. I know you did because, why would you come here? You wanted to get to know me too."

"I did, but now... ooh, I never want to see you again."

"Cara, please."

She went to the car, crying from the shock. Jocelyn noticed. The news about Jaime was too much for her to accept and hard to deny.

"What's wrong?" Jocelyn asked.

"I just want to go home."

"What happened?"

"You won't believe this. I can't even speak right now. Here's a shock, Jaime is not who I thought she was. She just told me she is my birth mom."

"What? And you believed her?"

"Her mail was addressed Sanderson. It was her married name."

"Oh, Cara. I don't know what to say."

"She also told me that your dad is her cousin."

"That means we are..."

"Second cousins. I need to talk to Dad."

They went home and Cara looked for him in his office.

"Dad, Dad come out here and talk to me!"

"Cara, what is it?"

"How did you meet Jaime?"

"She came highly recommended."

"Who recommended her?"

"I'm not sure why you're asking me this."

"Because I just talked to her at her house, and she revealed that she is my mother. Is that true?"

Derek took a moment to accept the shock Cara found out.

"Answer me!"

"It is true, Cara."

"You knew? Why did you and Jaime do this to me? I had family out there and no one bothered to find me when I was young? I spent all those years in foster care, and you never tried to find me."

"Your mother was not well enough to take care of you. I didn't know about you or where Jaime was until she reached out to me through a business partner I knew. I was out of town too much to take care of a baby. After I found you, Jaime and I decided I should adopt you. She was terrified you would reject her if you found out. She hated herself for giving you up. Her mother wasn't the best caregiver. She was blind as well and unable to care for her. I never got to see her until we were older. Your mother really wanted you back, but she was afraid the agency wouldn't give you back to her without a court hearing and then she would lose you forever. So, I adopted you. She wanted to see you, so I hired her to work on my property and tend to the horses. She has enjoyed watching you change and all you have become in your life. She just wanted a chance to see you. I am sure she was going to tell you." He moved over and put his hand on hers, "Cara, I know you love her."

She removed his hand, "No, I can't love her."

"But you do. Her stepping back to get to know you was a good thing. It gave her hope that you might love her no matter what happened in the past. I know so much has been going on in your life. I think you can put the past behind and move forward. Do you think you can forgive her?" Derek asked.

"No. How can I call you Dad?"

"It doesn't matter the status. We are a family. You can still call me Dad."

"Think of what this has done to Jocelyn."

"I will talk to her about it. The truth is, we all love you and we don't think about the mistakes we made. It's the here and now that matters. Real family stays close together."

Cara had a lot of thinking to do. She knew Derek was right. Their family dynamic was unique, but was there room for forgiveness? She laid there in bed closing her eyes, picturing her life with Jaime. She thought about the days she would look into the mirror and wonder what her mother looked like. A tear rolled off her cheek. She really had grown to love her mother. It was as if a force was pulling her to the woman who loved horses. Most of all, Jaime loved Cara.

Chapter 16

Desperation Turned To Love

Cara kept to herself after finding out that Jaime was her real mother. T.J. settled into his new place with Caleb. His new job was a perfect fit. After a few weeks he was offered more hours because of his skills. His company praised him more than he was expecting. The couple would talk briefly on the phone, but Cara's sadness always cut the conversation short. T.J. wished he could do more for her spirit.

Derek thought it was time to visit Jaime. He was concerned about his cousin because she had not been to the barn in a few weeks. Jocelyn and her boyfriend were taking care of the horses until she returned. Remarkably, Patrick had some experience taking care of sheep and goats on his grandfather's farm.

Derek walked up to Jaime's door. Through the screen he could see her door was open.

"Hi, Jaime. Can I come in?"

"Sure. I need a hug."

"You got it."

"How's Cara?" Jaime asked.

"Her vision is stable. We thought about the option to do surgery, but it would just buy us time."

"Is she thinking about me? I want to talk to her, but it still feels wrong."

"I know you do. She has been so quiet since then and on top of that she had to drop out of school. She is now having to use a cane to help her not bump into things."

"Remember when my mother always fell down? It was difficult for her to take care of herself and me," Jaime remembered.

"It seems like Cara's condition is hereditary. I miss the way she was when she could see. To me, she is still my daughter."

"Do you think what we did was wrong?" Jaime was feeling very guilty.

"I don't know. It was a blow, but I know how you felt when Matt died. I wish there were something I could have done sooner to help you and Cara in your situation. We know how foster care homes can be. Some good, some bad. Cara was fortunate enough to be placed in homes until she could come into her own. She is a gifted artist. Now, she's even given up on that."

"Is she totally blind?"

"No, she can see a little but it's blurry. The light bothers her, so she wears the sunglasses her doctor prescribed for her."

"I want to hold my daughter. I could feel so many times she wanted to hug me, and I resisted her out of fear. I pushed her away emotionally when I should have put my arms around her."

"I can understand why you were afraid. I am in your place. Even though it may not be fair, this was probably the best for Cara."

"I was too forceful in asking her to leave that day. I saw the look on her face and then I admitted to her that I was her mother."

"She will heal in time."

"How much time? When do I get my daughter back? I missed having her for over twenty five years."

161

"They have been getting their wedding plans finished. I had a talk with her, and I think she will come around to talking to you."

"When is the wedding?"

"August 20th."

"That's soon. Do you think I am still invited?"

"Of course. Cara would never uninvite you."

"I wouldn't blame her if she did."

"Now, I don't need two depressed women. It's going to be all right, I promise you. She will let you into her heart when the time is right."

Derek squeezed her hand as he left. He smiled at her giving her the reassurance the two would come together.

Jaime looked at the picture of her and Matthew. Because someone decided to get drunk and be stupid, his life ended and her whole life turned upside down. If she could do it all over again, she would have never given Cara away. The regret of a lonely mother set into her heart. She reflected on the thought of never getting those tender years back. After Derek had left, she went to a special place in her room where she kept memories of her family. There was a cabinet next to her closet that held the whole world she once knew. She took out a box, a wooden box made of Walnut. Opening it, she was uneasy. She hadn't opened it since Cara was born. She found the high school graduation picture of her and Matthew. He proposed at the top of a hill overlooking the beach that night. She didn't care if it was an elegant wedding or if they got married in their street clothes. She knew she found the one she wanted to be with. They had little money living in a studio house behind some property they rented from a local tree farmer. She wanted to have animals such as goats, chickens, and most of all, horses. Underneath some other photographs was Matthew's memorial invitation. They were married less than a year when he died. There were no other photos taken after he died. Her life ended the same day. Cara had colic and no longer wanted to nurse. Jaime was not able to pay rent or buy enough to eat. She couldn't sleep thinking about the desperation she was feeling. She thought of no other way to give her daughter a fighting chance.

After she ran out of the hospital, Jaime went back to her studio home to talk to her landlord. He forgave the amount of rent she owed and gave her the phone number of an elderly woman named Emmy who had been a horse trainer since she was sixteen. At eighty, she became unable to feed her horses and care for them. They met and Emmy gave Jaime a room to sleep in. She worked taking care of the barn, animals, their feed, and working with the vet to keep them healthy. From there, Jaime learned a lot about the environment she was falling in love with. Developing her skills helped her to forget the pain of deep loss. Because she was exhausted, every day she slept well at night. Emmy noted her working too much and begged her to slow down. That was not an option for her. She learned a way to cope. Ten years had passed, and Emmy had died in her bed. She left some money to Jaime. The house was sold and so were the horses. The anxiety of not knowing where her daughter could be was killing her inside. The guilt was not far behind.

On his own, Derek searched for Cara until he found that she was currently living with the Grier family. It was then that Derek decided to adopt her without involving Jaime. It took months to get all of the legal work completed. This family would get a second chance to heal an open wound. When Derek let his cousin know where her daughter was, hope filled her heart.

Out of all of the photos and cards in her box, none had the impact as the one she framed and put on her mantle. It was the last time she could remember that everyone she loved most were together. It was the day their family was complete. Everything that had happened since then had

163

been a foggy memory of desperation. Would she ever get it back?

Cara wanted to find it in her heart to forgive her mother. She grew to love her long before learning who she really was. She was unable to see the faces of those she loved. They were just a blur much like her past. She got up out of bed and grazed her hand across some of the art pieces she previously admired. They were all memories of a time when she colored her life. The many objects she drew told a story of what she grew up wanting. And what she wanted was a real mother, one she could see. Time was going by and before it was too late, she knew she had to reach out to her. Derek told Cara that Jaime was back at work.

"Where is she?" asked Cara.

"She's in the barn. Would you like me to take you to her?"

"Yes, please."

Derek held his daughter's hand and guided her to the barn.

"Jaime, you have a visitor."

"Hi. Are you glad to be back?" Cara asked timidly.

"Yes. I felt like I crawled back here after what happened to us."

"I'm still not right with it. But you're here and that is what matters now."

"I wanted to be there for you ever since I first came here. I wasn't trying to keep it a secret. I was protecting you and not thinking of myself."

"I know. I should have seen that. I wanted to hate you for what you did. I'm sorry I felt that way."

"I'm sorry about what I did. Tell me, were you happy growing up even if it wasn't with an ideal family?"

"I was at times. I did go to a home that was uncaring and the parents never warmed up to me. I asked to be moved but I had to just wait until I was placed with the Grier family. There is where I was the happiest."

"It makes me glad you had them. And now? How do you feel about how things are?"

"Better. These people are my real family. You are my family. I was thinking how I felt like a stranger here and I couldn't get Jane to love me. After I found you, I realized I am loved. I have my family here and especially; I have my mother back."

"I want to be part of your life, Cara. Can you find a place in your heart for me?"

"I have already put you there. Oh, Mother. Please hold me. I'm going blind and now that I found you, I will never see your face again."

"Cara, I love you. Yes, my love, I will hold you."

The two held on as if the wind was trying to bring them apart. There was love, true love for a daughter who was losing a fight to keep her sight. Jaime loved Cara during those times she was working at the barn. She wanted to hold her and tell her everything she was overflowing with. They no longer were torn apart by loss and the fear of the unknown.

Cara turned her head where the horses were. She could hear them.

"Did you miss them while you were away?"

"Yes I did. I used to do this silly thing since I was young to help them remember me."

"What was that?"

"I would blow on their nose and put my face near it so they could smell me. Bailey always comes to me because of it. Then she gives me kisses on my cheek. I love that."

"They're fortunate to have you."

"I am so glad to have you," Jaime said with tears in her eyes.

"It was too much for me to handle at the time. Now it's clear I want us to be close."

"What can I do to make it better?" Jaime asked.

"Being here is enough. It comforts me to hear your voice. I used to talk to myself in the mirror and pretend it was you, believing that we looked alike."

"You do look like me and your dad. Cara, I never meant to deceive you. Derek thought it would be a good thing to adopt you and the rest would come later. I didn't think it would be like this."

"All my other senses work harder since I have to concentrate on the things around me. Now that I know you're here to stay, I will miss looking at you."

"No matter what, you can always come to me."

"Do you know where Lindley Park is?"

"I do. I used to go there after your father died. But it was too heartbreaking to see moms with their children. At the time I couldn't be happy."

"That place was a safe haven for me. That's where I met T.J."

"And now are you safe? How are you feeling about us?"

"I want to start over. I need to take it slow. I want the hurt to go away"

"I want that too. I never stopped loving you, Cara."

Cara started to cry. Jaime approached her and touched her cheek softly.

"Here, let me have your hands," Jaime requested.

Cara put her hands out as Jaime held them. She raised them to touch the curves of her face.

"Look deep inside when you think about my face. Is this what you envisioned?"

"Oh, you are beautiful!" Cara discovered Jaime's identity with every touch.

With her other hand, Cara touched her own facial features to compare.

"It is so nice to meet you, Mother."

"Oh, Cara. It is wonderful to meet you."

Mother and daughter embraced, both with misty smiling eyes as they faced each other. The reward was given to Cara for waiting so patiently to give her mother love. Jaime led Cara over to her horse, Kindred.

"Come here. Touch his face," Jaime said.

Cara blew onto his face. The tender moment was a dream coming true for both Cara and Jaime. Cara shared her plans for the wedding. It was her wish for Derek and Jaime to walk her down the aisle on her special day. They talked for hours and learned more about each other. The pains, the hurt, the happy times and the bad. What was lost was now found. For Cara and Jaime, they emotionally walked miles to finally reach the light. Their roadway had become clearer. Their paths felt cleared of obstacles to stumble upon. For now, this was the best they ever had.

Chapter 17

The Long Road Ahead

The time came when Derek wanted to share his plans for his daughter and T.J. He had the family for a special dinner at the house.

"I would like everyone's attention. Our daughter, Cara will soon be a wife. She will be a complement to her husband all the days of their lives. We, as a family," he looked at Jane and nodded, "wanted to give our bride and groom-to-be a special gift. We are giving them a new home that we are building right here on our property. Congratulations to our growing family!"

"They got us a house!" Cara gasped.

"I wanted to live here with you," T.J. admitted. 'Thank you, Derek."

"Take care of her. She is worth it."

"I will."

Derek's contractors were working on T.J. and Cara's homesite. He took time to oversee the project to make sure every detail was perfect for his daughter. Safety for her condition weighed on his mind.

Cara was going to a school for blind learning new skills. It frustrated her to attempt Braille, cooking and even simple tasks. Jocelyn would stand by. Cara resisted asking for help even though her family didn't mind. She tried drawing again but that was going to be another skill that needed practice. She loved petting her horse but was still afraid to ride him. She had a visitor that came to help.

"Cara, it's Jaime."

"What a surprise. Are you working today?"

"Not today. I'm taking you riding."

"Oh, that's funny. I thought I heard you say you were taking me riding."

"I did. I talked to Derek and Jane, and they think it's time you got out there and rode Kindred again."

"I can't. You know my sight is nearly gone and it's just not the same."

"You're still the same. You know what to do. You trained hard for years. We have both been doing this for a long time. We could do it with our eyes closed. Today, you are going to ride your horse."

Cara knew Jaime wasn't going to take no for an answer. She reluctantly got into her riding clothes and Jaime walked her to the stables.

"What if he doesn't remember me?" Cara asked.

"You only lost your sight. I think he will know who you are."

Jaime led her to her horse.

"Touch his face. Put your hand on his mane."

"Hello, my friend. It's Cara."

"He knows you. Just breathe."

Kindred nuzzled Cara's cheek. He whinnied as she put her hand on his mane.

"He remembers, he really does."

"He's all saddled up for you. Jump up on your saddle and I'll walk by your side. It will be all right."

Jaime helped Cara climb onto her horse. She had to go back into her memory of those days when she rode for prizes and ribbons. She could remember the first day of

169

her competition, she was nervous and all she thought about was falling off. She had to use her training to get her through it. Jaime was a wonderful support for this past prize winner.

"We can do this every day and get you used to riding with me alongside you."

"After a few tries."

"Yes, when you are ready."

Cara felt her grip tighten on the reigns. Kindred nickered. Jaime wanted to relax her and started a conversation that would make this ride a favorite.

 "What is going through your mind?"

I love this about us. This was what I always wanted, you and me getting close. I shouldn't have made it so awkward and painful."

"I understood it wasn't going to be easy for either of us."

"Can you tell me more about my father?"

"Sure. He was kind. His family was not like mine. He had the whitest teeth, straight with a cute smile. His sandy colored hair covered his forehead. We were in the same class, and he sat behind me. He used to put his pencil in my hair. I was annoyed by it, but it was his way of getting my attention. After class, he asked if I'd like to have lunch with him. I just wanted to be his friend. He respected that and with time I grew to love him. He gave me a ring. It turned my finger green. He got it at a carnival he and his friends went to. It was one of those small prizes and he gave it to me. I wore that thing throughout high school. I had to wear it with a chain as a necklace since I couldn't get the green off my finger. I still have that old thing. He promised me he was going to marry me after school was over. We got married. It was a small wedding. I loved him so much, I wanted a child that looked just like him. We planned you and neither of us knew what to expect. When he saw you were his daughter, he was so happy. He was smitten for sure."

"Really?"

"He was. He worked hard for us. He came home tired working late into the night. The first thing he would do after he kissed me was to pick you up and talk to you. One night, he decided to take a different route home. It would get him home later, but he didn't want to be in traffic. Around the corner someone was in his lane. The drunk driver went to the hospital. Matt didn't. When I got the news from his dad, I lost my mind. We had no money saved and Matt's parents did what they could to help out, but I was too depressed to try and find work. Matthew was my life, breath, my love. Losing him killed any chance of being happy."

"I loved that picture you had of us together on your mantle. I think he was handsome."

"I see a lot of features in your face that look like him. It's like he's here when I see you."

"I'm happy to hear that."

"Let's get this horse to go for a trot."

"Are you sure? Not too fast."

"You know Kindred is the gentlest of all the horses here. Remember he knows you. We'll go slow."

It was true, she could feel her friend under her and learned to trust him. Jaime was going to train Cara all over again to ride without fear.

Patience made it easier for Cara to relearn everything, from things as simple as pouring milk to learning a new language. Things most humans take for granted were now tasks Cara had to remaster. There was still potential in her. With time, she would be doing well on her own, learning sightless. Jaime treasured her times with Cara. She would smile when her daughter told her how she used to imagine her a dancer or someone special. As Cara learned of Jaime's talent of horse handling, she grew prouder of her mother. She avoided thinking of herself as disabled. Losing one thing didn't mean she lost control of everything. She was loved and that was what she valued most. Jaime would visit every day and share her experiences and wisdom. She became her life teacher at home. There were many times of laughter, times when Cara needed to cry, times she needed to be held. Jane could have felt jealous over their relationship. But when she seen the effect, it was having on them both, she decided it was better for everyone. Cara still thought of Derek and Jane as her parents. Inside it felt better to have all three supporting her. Jaime would've said, "Like an old milking stool with three legs. The support is still there even on three." It was an unusual family dynamic, but it mattered more that they were family.

Jocelyn was in her room when Cara found her sitting on her bed, her phone by her side.

"Hey, are you busy? I can come back later."

"No, stay. Patrick had to go back to Ireland. He had a family emergency. His grandmother died and he had to be there."

"I'm sorry. Was he close to her?"

"Yes, very close. He said he will be back in a couple of weeks. I just got off the phone with him. What if he falls out of love with me?"

"If you sit here thinking that until he comes back, you'll be miserable."

"I don't want him to stay there."

"He'll be back. He needs to be there to be with his family."

"You sound like Jaime. You have been spending a lot of time with her."

"We are getting to know each other. I still can't believe you're my cousin," Cara laughed.

"Hey, we're a different kind of family. I like it."

"I was an only child, but I like having a sister and a cousin."

"How's school?"

"A pain. I can't get my brain to understand the Braille thing."

"Show me what you mean."

Cara took out her Braille book. The large book had the dots in their proper place. She guided Jocelyn's fingers across the page.

"Can you read any of this to me?" Jocelyn asked.

"I can. *The red ball is round.*"

"Pretty basic."

"Yeah, well, it's a start."

"I think it's great. You can read another language."

"You're right about that. It's complicated."

Cara heard her phone ring. It was T.J.

"Hello."

"Your dad said our house is getting painted in a couple of days. Are you ready for that?"

"Yes I am. I already talked to him about the color palette."

"That kitchen is open so you can get around better."

"I can't wait."

"Cara, I wanted to talk to you about something. I got a letter from my attorney. It's about Jackson."

"I thought we were through with that."

"We are, but he asked if I wanted to press charges."

"Are you going to?"

"I need to talk to Caleb about my options."

"You had closure. If this is what you want to do, you should go for it."

"I want him to never bother me again."

"You do what you think is best. I know you will."

T.J. was going to meet his attorney on the arraignment date. Jackson was in jail and might or might not be heading to prison. He didn't want to press charges out of spite, but he also had to protect his family. At the time, no one knew the fate of Jackson Perry.

Chapter 18

We Need Each Other

The new home was finally finished. Derek thought it would be a good idea for T.J. to move in. Cara used her white cane; a foldable one to help her get around without getting hurt. She visited her new home often to get a feel for it. She loved touching the walls and countertops. She walked through the hall and bedrooms smelling the fresh paint. T.J. would describe the furnishings that were soon to arrive and loved watching her smile. The house was designed just for her, spacious and easy to get around. Derek came over to talk to T.J. about the arraignment coming up soon.

"Hey, T.J. How are you feeling about the hearing?"

"Good, I guess. I have two of my best attorneys working on the case."

"Is Jackson in jail?"

"Yes. I want him to remain behind bars for a long time. I just don't know what justice has in store for me."

"He has a record. This might be bad news for him."

"I hope so. Cara is worried he will get out early and torture us. I don't want to think about that."

"I'm sure it will be okay. Caleb says they are gathering enough evidence to convict him," Derek said being reassuring.

"He's a good attorney."

"I just wanted to be sure you are okay. Your house turned out beautiful." Derek cared about T.J. very much. He was aware of the situation he grew up with and he needed family.

"I feel bad Cara can't see what we did for her."

"She will use her other senses to appreciate it. She seems okay with that. She's getting excited to move in after the wedding. Are you two planning a honeymoon?"

"I was thinking about that. Where do you take someone who can't see?"

"Think of what she would like. She loves the sounds and smells of the beach. Take her to The Bahamas. The feel of the salty air and the ocean might be what she needs after all she's been through."

"I think you're right. Thanks, Derek."

"Cara is sitting on the porch. Go talk to her."

T.J. wanted what was best for Cara, nothing less. For a woman who had been through so much, he felt everything should be perfect for her special day when she would finally come home to her own.

"Hey, honey. How are you today?"

"It's hard to know what to do when you can't see the world anymore. There are times I want to just scream and ask why. Somedays, I'm fine with it. I had a meeting with the counselor at my school today."

"What did she say?" T.J. queried.

"She wanted to be sure I was not depressed. She said she noticed I was looking discouraged in class. I was. The more sight I lose, the worse I feel. Why can't I just accept it?"

"It must be a difficult thing to lose. Does it feel like you have to learn everything all over again?"

"I feel like a helpless baby, then I get my birth mother back into my life and what happens? I can't see her face anymore. I feel like a little kid who always needs help."

"You still have a lot of skills that you've learned. You just have to use them differently."

"Everything is better when you are here."

"That's good. You are in a better place. You still have your memories and if we have any children, you will make memories with them even if you can't see."

"Now I know you walked over here to talk to me about something."

"How do you know that? Did I give a hint I wanted a conversation?"

"You asked if I was alright? That's a sure clue you want an answer to something."

"Well, you're right about that. I was talking to your dad about going on a honeymoon. You know, some place special you would like to go. He recalls you saying how much you like the beach."

"I do. Oh, don't tell me you want to go to the San Diego beach, maybe, Oceanside."

"No, no. I was thinking some place you have never been to before. The Bahamas. How does that sound?"

"I think I'd like that. I heard that the sand and ocean are so warm. Is that where you want to go?"

"Yes. I think I would love to honeymoon with you on the Caribbean."

She stood up to touch his face, something she did regularly to connect with those she loved.

"Someday I will learn all the curves of your face and body," she said as she stroked his facial features.

"I will always be here."

T.J. led her into her parent's house to get something to eat. They heard Jaime drive up.

"Oh, I wonder what she is doing here."

"I don't know."

"Hello, everyone," Jaime announced.

"Hello, Mom. What's going on today?"

"I'm here to see Jane."

"I think she's in the house."

"She's expecting me. We are going to do something together."

"Well, have fun. T.J. is moving into the new house."

"Oh, that's great news. I should go take the tour."

"Do you have a few minutes? I can take you now," T.J. suggested.

"Sure, let's go. Cara, will you tell Jane that I'll be back?"

"Okay."

"Did I hear Jaime?" Jane said.

"Yes. She went to tour the house. Where are you two going?"

"We just need some time to have a mom conversation. I mean, we both share a daughter. A friend of mine owns a ranch caring for abandoned farm animals. I love the work they do at that place. We raised a lot of money to help those poor animals. I thought Jaime would like to go check it out."

"Are you going to get to know her better?"

"I think I should."

"I like having two moms. I know you'll like her."

"What are you doing today?" asked Jane.

"Sometimes I get so angry. There was so much I wanted to do, and I just found my mother. Now I am limited as to what I can do on my own. I feel like I have to use my brain more, like working a new muscle."

"It could be like exercise. I think you're going to be good at it once you learn. You will have more time with your mother than you realize. Soon enough, your lifestyle will be adjusted to your condition. What do you like to do even if you cannot see?"

"Play piano. I used to close my eyes when I was younger to see how good I knew the music."

"Yes, you do that very well. Would you play something for me before they come back?" Jane asked.

Jane wanted to boost her confidence knowing six years of practice should pay off. Cara helped herself to the bench and began to play Beethoven's Moonlight Sonata. When Jaime walked into the house, she saw her daughter playing with such grace and beauty. It took her breath away to hear such beautiful music. When she was done, Jamie felt moved from her talent.

"Cara, that was so beautiful!" Jaime expressed.

"The one thing I can do blind. Thank you, Jane for making me take all those lessons."

"It's true. Young people only appreciate the arts later in life."

"Are you ready to go?" Jane asked Jaime.

"Sure."

It was good to see Jaime and Jane becoming a family. This was something she wanted while she kept her identity a secret. It would give them a chance to get to know each other better.

"Cara, you have a real gift," T.J. complimented.

"I do love to play. I stopped practicing once my sight was deteriorating."

"I think we should get you a piano for our home so you can play anytime you want."

"I have been trying to draw my art pieces but that's going to take more practice."

"Have you ever thought about teaching, maybe to children?"

"No. Do you really think I could?"

"I think you can. You think about it while I prepare lunch for us."

Cara didn't know what she was going to do for a job. The idea of being a piano teacher sounded appealing. Instead of the frustrations she was experiencing, maybe this was a better way to look at things. Cara had the ability to help others. Confidence began to fill her mind again.

Jaime thought it would be a good idea to talk to Jane about the relationship she would love to have with her family. Jane knew Derek had a cousin that he was separated from her during their younger years. She didn't know Jaime was his relative or why they decided to keep the adoption search for Cara a secret. Jane wanted more information about Jaime and where she fit into Cara's life.

"I'm glad we get to talk," Jane said.

"I would like to get to know you better. I know it has been a rough adjustment over the years. I apologize for that."

"Derek has never kept anything from me. When he told me he wanted to adopt a young girl for Jocelyn, I didn't like the idea. I just wasn't ready to take on another child. Jocelyn was lonely, I knew that. Some of that was my fault."

"Families have their problems. You and I have similar situations. I think as a family we can be there for Cara. You are her mother legally. I am her birth mother, and I would never get in the way of what you and Derek have built. I just want to be involved in her life."

"It has been a long road trying to mend the mistakes I made with my girls. I decided to get help outside of my family and talk to a therapist. I need help with the frustrations I have been carrying for so many years."

"Sounds like Derek was our saving grace. I believe we will all heal from what we did and what you went through."

"When I found out the handler he hired was the mother of Cara, I was upset. After a while, I realized why you two kept this from me."

"I know. I had to get ready to be her mother again. I had so many changes to make in my mind and heart. It took me a long time to recover from Matthew's death. I thought I was going to die from the pain. Are you glad we are here now, and we can heal together? Are you happy I am in your life?" Jaime asked.

"I am now. I think I prejudged you. I couldn't understand what made you give her away."

"It's complicated. I didn't know all the reasons either. I was not in my right mind. I had no other family and later I searched for Derek to help me. He was working on his business, and he didn't know where I was at the time."

"I know what we have experienced is not what most families go through. The fact is you really are a wonderful person."

"So are you. Can I ask, why was it so hard for you to love your daughter, Jocelyn?

Jane didn't know how to answer that question. Derek assured her she was able to show her child love, but she was uncomfortable, thinking it might not be possible for her.

"I didn't know how to love a child. I didn't know how to love Derek at first. Even after we got to know each other better, I doubted whether I could give him the love he needed. There wasn't much of that where I came from."

"Is that why you chose to give to others through your charities?"

"It distracted me. I was overly consumed with myself, my feelings, my life. I could only take care of myself and keep safe from getting hurt. Derek made it easy to trust. Even when I had a breakdown, he was calm and patient with me."

"He was like a brother to me. I was an only child like him. Our dads were brothers. His father was successful, mine was cold. He avoided any affection from me or my blind mother."

"That does explain Cara's condition."

"Yes. When she told me she was going blind, I wanted to run into her arms at that moment, but I was afraid she would push me away forever. That feeling was worse than when I left her at that hospital."

"How are you now about it?"

"Happier, better. I think I healed slow, but I was okay it was gradual. Being here with Derek's horses and getting to know her helped me in so many ways to love again."

"Where are we now? What do I mean to you, being Cara's adopted mother?"

"I knew you had it rough, Jane. I noticed it and I was afraid you would hurt her, and you did. She couldn't imagine getting close to you."

"I'm sorry for that. To be honest, I only wanted to love Derek, no one else for the rest of my life. Who does that? Who doesn't let others in who want to love you? I guess it was all about trust."

"I can see you are making efforts to try."

"Does it make you think differently about me and how I have raised Cara?"

"No. I could only think of how it felt and that it was too late for me. You were fortunate to have her with you, and you wanted to do what was best for her."

"I pushed her like I pushed myself. Derek made me think when he grew tired of how much I forced Cara into riding. She really hated those piano lessons."

"Now, she loves it. Don't think you were bad for her. I'm glad she learned because of you."

"What? Jaime, I am so glad to hear you say that. From anyone outside my family, I never had validation. I needed to hear that."

"Jane, think about what you have done for all the charities you sweat and toiled over. You worked very hard to get to where you are. You raised a lot of money for needy families, you walked for Breast Cancer Awareness, you made donations with your own money. Look at all you do for others."

Jane looked down as she began to cry. There was a gap that needed to be filled with her family's love. Jane covered her sadness when it was her unselfishness that made her a good mother. She wanted it to show, but failure frightened her and made her aggressive. Jaime grew fond of Jane. She realized what she was going through. Her feelings were showing empathy for the pain Jane was keeping deep inside of herself. Jaime took her hand and let her cry as she started to speak to her.

"Jane, this is a breakthrough for you and me. I see you, who you really are. We can support each other so we can be good parents for Cara and any grandchildren that may come. You are here with me, and I will always be here for you."

"Thank you. I never had a close friend to tell my troubles to. I hope therapy will help me face the trauma and become a better mom."

"You are on your way. What I like about you is that you keep getting back on the horse."

They embraced as if they were long lost sisters who loved each other at first glance.

"Jaime, we need each other. We are a family and it's never too late to love. Forgiveness is here to stay."

"I'm so glad we talked. Now, I need a tour of this remarkable ranch."

"My pleasure."

From then on, they found what they needed to cope with any challenges they would face in the future. Instead of feeling sad about Cara, they would treat her with love, knowing she would find her way through her new life. Jane relied on Jaime and that was okay with her. It was good to have a listening ear anytime she felt she wasn't good enough. In time, things improved and continued. Love lives on between two women who needed each other.

Chapter 19

It Happens When I Think Of You

The time finally came when T.J. attended the arraignment for Jackson John Perry. He had been in jail for sixty days, serving out his time for some of the crimes he committed. Caleb and his assistant accompanied T.J. into the courtroom.

"Hey, how are the nerves?" asked Caleb.

"I'm good. I thought I would never see his face again and now he has to appear before us."

"Don't sweat it. It will be alright. He's the one in the hot seat."

Jackson entered into the courtroom in shackles in an orange prison outfit. He looked mangled and beat. Sitting next to his appointed attorney, he was asked not to speak until all the evidence was out in the open.

"All rise. The Honorable Judge Campbell presiding," stated the bailiff.

The judge listed the many counts of abuse and assault. Armed robbery and several warrants were presented.

"Jackson Perry how do you plea?" the judge asked.

His attorney told the judge he pleads no contest. This meant there would have to be a trial to determine his fate. He was hoping for a lighter sentence. The attorney knew he wouldn't get a slap on the wrist for his aggravated crimes.

"Mr. Bryan Dawson, you have decided to press charges on Mr. Jackson Perry?" asked the judge.

"Yes sir."

"Do you have anything to say to Mr. Perry?"

"Yes. Jackson, because you made a mess of your life, you decided to try to cause chaos in mine. You are deceiving, a liar, a thief, a hardened soul that never deserved my mother and all the patience she had with you. Then you came into my home and demanded I cower to you, to bow down and wince before you. I shall not do such a thing, in the name of my mother, Ella Carolyn Dawson, I hope nothing in your life is easy. Today, I hope to get justice for how cruel you were to me as a child and how you tricked my mother into letting you be a part of our lives. Whatever happens to you, you will remember this day. The day I put the thoughts and traumas I experienced to rest. I defeated the dragon that you are and will always be."

T.J. went to sit beside Caleb.

"That was awesome!" said Caleb.

"I just want justice. I can barely breathe. It's a lot to take in."

After the judge spoke about how Jackson didn't care about anything and he refused to respond saying, "I have nothing to say," they took Jackson away until further notice of a trial date. T.J. shook Caleb's hand and walked out of the courtroom and fell onto his knees in the hallway. He was in tears thinking about how much his mother would have been proud of him. He was a true hero and a son who had a chance to get justice he deserved. Jackson didn't care if he went to prison. T.J. was granted a permanent restraining order from Jackson. He knew now he was finally safe from the evil that sat in that courtroom looking stoic when he was told there was going to be a trial. Geoff was later convicted as well.

After coming home, Caleb decided to spend the night with his friend in case he needed some support. Derek saw him come home and walked Cara over to him.

"How did it go?"

"It went very well. We have to go to a trial. we got a permanent restraining order against him," Caleb explained.

'T.J., how are you?" Derek asked.

"Spent. That was emotional and difficult. We were in court for over an hour."

"When is the trial?" Derek asked.

"We aren't sure yet." Caleb said.

"I never knew being in court could be so exhausting."

"Caleb, how do you do it?" Derek asked.

"My dad was an attorney, so I guess it's because I grew up around it. My dad always wanted me to stand up for justice."

"Hey, can I have a few minutes with Cara?"

"Sure, buddy," said Caleb.

"Come on, Caleb. How about a drink?" Derek led him into the den.

Cara put her hand on T.J.'s shoulder and then in his hair. She was hoping her compassion would go deep into his heart and he could gain some comfort.

"I don't know where I would be without you or if I came home to no one. What would become of me if I didn't have you?"

"I never want to imagine what that would feel like."

"To see him there in that courtroom, looking like the nothing he is and hearing his voice just sickened me."

"T.J. how can we get past this?"

"I'm going to let some time do the healing. Right now, I want my mother here. I would be stressed with this kind of news, and she would want to celebrate. I fell to my knees hearing her voice in my head that she was proud of me."

"There is no place I would want to be but here with you. You gave me comfort many times and now I want to return the love you showed me. You have me here for support during everything we go through."

"I needed to hear that. What I went through every day killed any hope I had that I would escape my pain and hurt. Hearing those fights, the screams, and all the aches I suffered as an innocent child. I gave my speech to the judge, and I let out all my pain until it was over. Mom is no longer with me, but there is you. I feel like I could fly, like I have wings because of it. It happens when I think of you. I wasn't just bruised at the heart; I was harmed physically. This was final and I knew I would come home to you. Here with you, I am home. I am safe, I am in love, I have justice. My mother's death can now rest, and I know that he will never hurt me again," he sighed deeply.

Cara knew T.J. said it all. She couldn't speak. With her by his side, he could move on from it. She would make his life fulfilling. Nothing would be impossible for them because of their love.

T.J. just held on to her, in the quiet, knowing they were able to understand each other. The healing was taking place for the young boy who wished for the best life a kid ever wanted. T.J. had all the riches he could possibly want; Cara's love and strength would get him through their years together.

The trial was set, and T.J. spent another exhausting day in court. After hearing both sides of their sworn statements, a verdict was finally ready to be heard. Jackson Perry was found guilty on all charges and restitution was paid to T.J. for his pain and mistreatment of abuse. He would spend the rest of his days in prison for serious felonies. The verdict would close the chapter of the wanton abuse that shouldn't have occurred in the life of Bryan Dawson.

Making new memories with Cara would keep those bad days at bay. He was no longer the trapped kid, curled up in the corner of his bedroom listening to his mother cry or having to fear a man who was no more than a monster. It was over and he had his power back.

Chapter 20

The Darkness Came

The day came when Patrick returned from Ireland. He gathered inspiration from his home country to ask Derek to put some sheep on a part of his pasture. He was a professional sheep shearer and learned to care for them while on his grandmother's farm. Derek observed his daughter watching Patrick outside with the horses. Derek considered sheep because of Patrick's passion for these gentle animals. He wanted to make his daughter happy and with Patrick's help, they began to make it happen.

Jocelyn looked over at Cara sitting alone on the porch as she often did. She tried to understand how she was feeling. She had approached her many times to get a smile from her, but it looked like her joy of life was dimming again. It seemed like one week she was optimistic and the next was in deep despair. This time, Jocelyn was moved to pull her sister out of her emotional darkness.

"Cara, why do you sit here every day? Please come be with us in the barn."

"What will I do in the barn? Just sit there like I am doing right now?"

"You need to live. Losing your sight changes nothing about how we feel about you."

"You can see the sunsets, you get to see Patrick, you can see. You will never know what this is like for me."

"That is very true. We were all saddened by it. We have to move on from that and live. You have so much to live for. I know you will adjust, and it won't always be this hard."

"You really think so? I miss seeing T.J.'s face, I miss running through our fields and watching the horses enjoy the beauty of these pastures. What good am I now that I am broken?"

"You keep saying that as if it's hopeless and you use that as an excuse to stay in your little world of pity. We don't feel sorry for you, we love you."

"I look at your face and you are just a blur of cloudy images. I try to adjust it. I close my eyes and it's still there. I want to see the color of my children's eyes. I want to see the world."

"I know. It's hard to accept. You will have a family; you will use your other senses to love your children. You can't give up so easily. This is why you enrolled at the school for the blind. You will learn."

Cara felt like she was completely helpless and paralyzed. She realized that what she was going through was not improving quickly, if at all. She could hear the desperation in her sister's voice. Jocelyn reached out to touch her hand. Cara's focus easily fell on the negative parts of her life. It was going to take some time to recover from all the loss that kept returning. Shadows and colors were dimming fast. There were noticeable bruises on her legs from bumping into objects. She was running out of reasons to return to her family and repair her life.

"Cara, the man I met, and love works harder than anyone I know. He has been through so much in his life and he never lets that stop him from living. I love him for that. T.J. never judged you or stopped loving you, the real you inside. You will grow from this. Think about how much love there is right in front of you."

Cara put her arms out to hold Jocelyn. She was grieving and was in fear of the time when she would be living in complete darkness. Her battle needed to come to an end. Jocelyn would do anything for Cara but getting her to live again was something Cara had to do on her own.

T.J. didn't like watching his love wallow in sadness. Even at work his mind tried to formulate ways to help. He came up with an idea that might bring out the person he knew years ago.

"Has she been sitting there all day?" asked T.J. to Jocelyn.

"Yes. I tried talking to her and I think she wants to accept things as they are but she's afraid."

"I think I have a solution. It may not work but I want to try."

"What is it?"

"I want to take her to the place she loves."

"I'm hoping that it works. She has so much life in her."

T.J. came over to Cara.

"Cara, please stand up."

"Why?"

"You and I are going someplace. You won't need your sight where I am taking you."

T.J.'s love for Cara went beyond the sacrifices anyone would make when they loved someone. He would give up everything for her. As the car came to a stop, he helped her out.

"Where are we?" she asked.

Instead of answering her, he walked her past the benches to the tree where their love first began. She could hear the birds.

"Put your hand on this, and wait here," he instructed.

T.J. climbed up where their initials were carved.

"Cara, you were standing right there when I asked you to come up with me, remember?"

"I remember."

He spoke to her while she was standing there. She started to smile.

"You're so silly. Aren't you too old to be in that tree?"

"No. I would do anything for you, even make a fool of myself."

"What?" she laughed.

"Anything." While in the tree, he shouted out.

"Anyone who can hear my voice, I want you to know that I love this woman. She has the most beautiful eyes and is more perfect than ever and I am in love with her!"

He wanted Cara to feel loved. He did everything he could to show it.

"And this is our tree!" he added.

As he climbed down, he looked into her eyes and took her hand. She could see his muddled form in front of her.

"Why did you do this for me?" she asked.

"I would do anything for you. I fell in love with you and everything you give your heart to. I am aware that you are losing your sight. That's okay. I love your eyes, not your sight. My love for you goes beyond any changes we meet along the way."

She was trying to regain her hope that losing sight stole from her. She had the best thing in her life standing in front of her. He was giving all his love to the woman who never expected to meet her true love. He was perfect for her, and she knew it. There at the park, in front of everyone watching, he danced with her and sang. When they stopped, she put her hand at the back of his neck and rested her face on his shoulder. She felt like a child being rocked with a comforting embrace. There they were, the two of them ready to take on the journey of being one with each other. Cara was ready to give herself to T.J. by becoming his wife someday.

They drove home after a long afternoon together. She went to bed not thinking about her sight. She could let it rest for the day.

Morning came and Cara could hear everyone waking up. Her hearing was heightened, and she noticed noises more than she used to. As she opened her eyes, she discovered a frightening truth. She started to breathe faster; anxiety went through her body. She walked around trying to touch anything to keep her from falling. She touched her eyes and rubbed them to regain any blurred images. They were not coming, and it caused her to do the only thing she could think of to release her fear. She called for her father.

"Dad, Dad help me!" Cara was screaming.

Derek came into Cara's room. Jocelyn followed him in.

"Cara, what is it, dear?" He was holding her as he looked at the distress on her face.

"It's dark, it's so dark. I can't see anything. It's too dark. I'm afraid."

"I'm here, I'm right here," Derek comforted.

Derek looked over at Jocelyn while he helplessly held her trembling in his arms.

"Make it go away. I want to see again. Please help me," she cried.

Jocelyn stood next to Cara touching her hand. This family was at the realization that Cara was fully blind sooner than unexpected.

"Call T.J. Ask him to come here!," Derek asked of Jocelyn.

"Okay."

Derek held Cara like she was a little girl. He could feel that she was emotionally helpless, and her total darkness frightened her. He said nothing as she wept in his arms.

T.J. ran over as soon as he could to be by her side.

"Son, hold her. She is in darkness. We were not prepared for it to come so soon. She needs you more than ever," Derek relayed.

T.J. looked at Cara and couldn't believe it finally came. Cara could no longer see any images, color or light.

"Cara, I'm here. It's going to be alright. I will always be here."

"T.J. I'm afraid of the dark."

"We will get through this together."

The next day, they called the school counselor asking her to come to see Cara to help with her adjustment. He feared she might get too depressed to move on with her life. When the counselor arrived, Cara was tired from crying and sat in her room facing the wall.

"Cara, it's Lisa from the blind school. Can we talk?"

"What is there to talk about? I can't see you or my family anymore."

"I can help you get through this. Please let me help you."

"I'm afraid."

"I know. We can work together, and you will live a normal life again. Would you like that?"

"I don't know what I want."

"We can help you with that. I would like you to come to the school today. Let's get you started in being more productive."

195

Lisa watched Cara get dressed and walk around the house, not relying on anyone to help her. Derek wanted to help Cara and Lisa put her hand out to say no. Cara walked to the bathroom to brush her teeth and her hair. Lisa told Cara where her cane was, and she walked into the kitchen. Lisa instructed Cara on how she could use the kitchen.

"Why aren't you helping me?" Cara asked.

"You can help yourself. You've done all this before with a little sight. You need to learn to do things for yourself without it. You can do it."

"I'm afraid."

"It's time to stop being afraid. We can go slow but you have been partially blind for quite some time. Use what you have learned so far."

With practice, Cara would master being a capable woman. This was the start of many months of learning to get around and get her life back. Looking back, she remembered the shock of being in darkness. She realized how similar it was to the time when she was abandoned. Each time she moved away from one home to another left a void of darkness. Time had to pass to get through another storm of the unknown. There were memories of her favorite colors and family photos locked in her mind. She never lost what she once had, it was just out of her reach. Lisa became a positive mentor for Cara. They developed a friendship that took her to the next level of learning to live in her new world.

The one person Cara was anxious to be with was Jaime. She was aware of Cara's new condition. She should understand what she was going through since Jaime's mother was also blind.

"Lovely one, I'm here," said Jaime.

"Mother." Cara held out her hand.

"I heard about what happened. I'm so sorry. I wish this were happening to me instead of you."

"No. I need to accept it. I'm so glad you are here."

"I wanted to come sooner, but I wanted to give you some time. I know you needed time."

"I was feeling sorry for myself. Everyone tried hard to show how much they loved me, and I rejected it. I became very negative. Now, I am in total darkness, and I am being shown how my life is full of blessings. You are one of those blessings."

"I want to be in your life with or without sight. I have so much love to give and it's all for you."

"I had it in my heart to forgive you for abandoning me as a baby. It's like the darkness has wiped away the old and I need to start with the new. I'm happy we found each other before I became blind."

"I am glad to have found you too."

Their fingers intertwined as Cara touched her mother's hands. There was nothing that could separate them from what they have become to each other. Cara was alive and grateful for Jaime. She was an adult who knew how to love because it was built inside of her through Jaime. Through all the pain and agony of loss, there was forgiveness and the opportunity to regain love at its finest. Cara found that love. She found it with Jaime and the family she belonged to. There was love out there that wanted to find her. The time had to be right, and it didn't matter anymore when Jaime and Cara found each other. They were living in the moment where a mother could hold the daughter she never stopped loving.

Cara and her family decided to honor her and welcome her blindness. They gathered out near the pasture and T.J. had doves in a cage. He wanted to let Cara know she was truly accepted and loved by those who knew her good heart. They all held hands as T.J. let the doves go. It was a symbol of letting go of the past. A new life was starting for Cara and T.J. Now that Cara had released her pain, she could finally embrace the life she always wanted.

Weeks had passed since the day those doves were released. It was time to make Cara a wife. Months of planning had finally come to an end. Cara was able to plan her dream wedding before she lost her sight. She remembered everything her and Jocelyn put together with Jane's help. Jocelyn was in her room when Cara was standing in front of her feeling the lace on her wedding dress.

"Are you ready to do this?" Jocelyn asked.

"I am. I never thought this day would come. You were with me the whole time no matter what was going on in my head."

"I wanted to be there for you. Do you need help getting your dress on?"

"No. Just help me zip it afterwards."

Jocelyn watched her sister put on her dress. Her hair, makeup, and veil looked stunning with the dress complementing the whole ensemble. Cara and T.J.'s day was going to be the most memorable day of their lives. Cara no longer felt like she lost control. She was surrounded by the family who knew how to love through any obstacle or storm. This was her day to shine through the darkness.

Chapter 21

I Knew You Were The One

The guests had gathered for the wedding that was carefully planned. Jane was sure that each detail was perfect. Pink and white roses dressed the tables with Spode China and fluted glasses for Cristal champagne. Cara's favorite chocolates were put in dishes for the guests. Magnolia trees were placed behind the tables where the gifts would rest. Candles flickered a romantic light on the tables for the bride and groom. Guitar music played in the background. The wedding would take place at sunset.

Cara wanted to go barefoot since walking in heels was not comfortable. T.J. persuaded Caleb to be his Best Man.

"If it wasn't for you, this may not have been possible," T.J. admitted to Caleb.

"I would never let anything happen to you, man. You're my best friend. You were always like a brother to me."

Jaime came into the dressing area to see her daughter in her beautiful dress.

"Cara, you look lovely."

"Thank you. I can only remember what it looked like when I could see better. Is it lacy enough?"

"It sure is. No dress can be as pretty as this!"

"How's Derek, I mean, Dad?"

"He's a nervous wreck. He can't wait to walk you down that aisle."

"What are you wearing?"

"A chiffon Balenciaga. Jane ordered it for me. To be honest, I would have been just as happy in jeans and chaps," Jaime joked.

"T.J. and I want to ride horses for our wedding photos. Jocelyn is taking our photos."

"She's been pretty happy since she met Patrick. I think your dad could be planning another wedding soon. Everyone likes him."

"He's so good with the animals. I like him, too."

"Me too."

Cara reached out her hand to hug her mother.

"Are you ready?"

"Yes. Let's go."

Jaime walked her out where Derek was going to meet her. They both took her by the arm and led her down the aisle. Cara couldn't see T.J. but she didn't care. As Derek handed her over to him, T.J. whispered, "Are you ready to begin our life?"

"Our life begun when we met. I am ready for a new journey. I wish I could see you. I'm sure you look handsome."

"You look beautiful in your bare feet."

Both wanted to say something to each other before taking their vows. T.J. went first.

"Cara Jo Sanderson, when I was fourteen years old, I had a dream to run away from pain and fear. I saw you each day at the park. You were so beautiful. I never felt that way about any girl before. I had to get up enough courage to ask you to climb the tree and carve something with me. I knew you were the one for me. I will forever be grateful for your caring, kind, and loving treatment. In our hearts

200

there was only us. No matter what you've been through, no matter your past, I will always love you, respect you, and cherish every moment we are together. I love you."

"Bryan Dawson, T.J., I will never forget that day we met. You pulled me out of my discomfort and brought me up to where we could be together. I was a child and felt very alone. I was looking for my mother who is now here with us on our special day. My wish has come true and I have been found by you. You have taken me into your life and heart and made everything new with enough love to go around. My dreams have come true before my eyes. Even though my sight is gone, nothing will change how I feel. T.J., today I give you my strength, my love, everything I possess. Today, you will be my husband. I love you."

After taking their vows, and sealing it with a kiss, the couple turned toward their close friends and family. T.J. Holding hands, Cara turned to T.J.

"Did we just get married?" she asked smiling.

"We sure did, Mrs. Dawson."

When it came time to dance with his wife, T.J. held her close and swayed with her while she rested her cheek on his shoulder. She felt the music. Her body took in the emotion she wanted for her first dance with her husband. The sound of the music was perfect. Her sister joined with Patrick next to them. She never wanted the night to end.

Though Cara lost her sight indefinitely, nothing would make her feel like that day was not the greatest day of her life. Her family was not lost. She had found her mother and she was bonded to the love of her life.

On the way to their honeymoon, they sat next to each other, her hand in his.

"Cara, I want to say something to you. That day I saw you near the tree at Lindley was the day I will not forget even when we grow old. No one would ever understand what that meant to me. Someone could go through loss, abuse, feeling like there was no way out, and be hopeless. I stopped feeling that way the day I saw your face. This beautiful face." He held her chin, "Sweet, beautiful Cara Jo who looked up when I called out to you. Suddenly, I felt like the prince up in the tower. We both needed rescuing."

"You are my prince. You are everything I wanted. Some people may think that they don't need anyone to share life with. Being alone gave me a reason to pretend I was loved. I would imagine that my mother was near me, hearing her voice, feeling her gentle touch as she held me. But it was you. Thank you for asking me to climb up. Thank you for helping me feel safe. I wrote something for you." She pulled out a folded paper. "It's probably messy. Will you to read it to me?"

"Okay."

T.J., I wrote this letter to express what it means for me to meet someone who needed rescuing as much as I. I'd close my eyes before I fell asleep. I had a thought. I would come find you, looking everywhere I thought you might be. I look up at a window in an apartment. I believe in my heart it is where you are. I run to you, out of breath trying to get to you. I take your hand asking you to come with me. You hesitate but I am persistent. I want to take you away from the pain you are suffering. I want to take you away from Jackson. It was my dream every night. I was sad when I couldn't take you away and there was nothing I could do to stop it. For years, I kept thinking about you, where you were, why you stopped writing me, were you happy? I mourned the loss of a friend. I came to Lindley Park to relive our memories. I pictured you there, calling out to me. Every day I came by. It was you; it was you who was there at the very bench where I used to sit. In my heart, I hoped it was you again. Now I stand before you on the day I became your wife, I am grateful I never gave up looking for you. In my dream when you hesitated, you told me you wanted to go but you couldn't. I asked why and you opened your door wider and pointed to the woman who protected your childhood, Ella. You wouldn't leave without her. She needed you to carry her through her hardest times. When she passed away, it was time to let go and I found you again. You were ready. It's put to rest and bad memories were part of your past. It never defines who you are. Your strength made me fall in love with you. My love, I have lost my sight. I will never see our children or the flowers in our garden. I will never see my mother's face, except in my mind. My hands will be my eyes, touching each curve so I do not forget you. You kept me in your thoughts while you were away. You said you would never forget me, and you held on to that promise. I am secure knowing you will never leave my side. Blindness has not made me resentful but has made me happy to have a family who is whole, together, and loved. Thank you, my love, for being there when there was little hope. Thank you for bringing the light to me until the dimness faded its beauty. I see you better without my eyes because my heart will always see your devotion to me, Bryan Dawson, my husband. Your Love Always, Cara Jo Dawson

T.J. held Cara's hand while he read to her. Her eyes were closed. Then he spoke to her.

"Cara, I have never read anything so touching and warm. How you feel about us is the most beautiful thing. It is something you feel, not see."

She touched his face and smiled. The time they had alone was going to be the memory they would hold onto. T.J. put the letter in a frame in their room near their wedding picture. Theirs was a love that would last a lifetime. In her mind, she was locked in. She wanted to stay in that moment. It was more than just an emotional high. She was his and that was all that was important to her.

Chapter 22

We Touched The Sky

Cara sits in her favorite chair and remembers how her family grew after their wedding almost three years ago. Her bare feet love the feel of the wool rug beneath them. Memories return to her of life on her parents' property.

Nine months after Cara's wedding, Jocelyn and Patrick had married and bought a piece of land for themselves next to her father's property. Jocelyn never imagined she would love farming as much as Patrick. She loved watching the sheep in the pasture after they had been shorn. New lambs with long bouncing tails were born. New colts and foals learned to stand and run. Jocelyn loved taking pictures of all of it. She continued some side jobs in photographing weddings and baby showers and would often fill Cara in on her latest projects.

Soon after her honeymoon, Cara started teaching. She loved the children who came to her home to take piano lessons. Music would fill the room.

"I hate these lessons," one red-haired student complained.

"I used to say the same thing when I was young. You only think that way now. Believe me, you'll be glad you worked hard at it when you grow up."

"I doubt it."

Cara would just grin.

Jane was standing close enough to hear while visiting at Cara's home. She thought of all of those times when Cara's own lessons were not easy. Jane's heart was always touched to hear Cara's mastery of the piano and was equally proud of how she shared her gift with others. Cara had joy in her life and exuded joy to others. Having a family of her own was not far off. The children who took lessons from her adored her. She was likeable and endearing with a gentle side. She could relate to what they were thinking, knowing any lessons could be frustrating. She always knew how to love. Cara thought about having children of her own.

Cara didn't need her sight to feel complete. It was a difficult four years learning to deal with her imperfection, but it felt like she had everything to make up for that. She had Jaime, the mother she longed for. She had T.J. Nothing was perfect but at a young age Cara found a rescuer. It was what she needed at the time. However, Cara realized she no longer needed to be rescued. She was doing fine on her own and blindness came easy to her with its adjustment. She smiled more, she loved her life and was ready to take on motherhood.

T.J. was a big part of those years. She sits and pictures his love as the curtains of a waterfall flowing over her and washing away her fears. There is nothing like him in the world as far as she is concerned. There is no one else who could understand like him. Still vivid in her mind, she sees him. She had looked up when he called to her. She climbed up trusting him where he felt safe. These are her memories she will keep.

His face is imprinted in her mind and at night when saying goodnight, she pictures him looking into her eyes. She recalls turning the pages of his tender letters and rests her hand on them, reading them over and over in her mind to help her sleep. She wants to grow old with him, kiss him every morning, love him every day. She will always treasure their memories. She was glad to have these before the darkness came.

Jaime is riding her horse just before sunset. It is her pattern. Her long hair blows behind her and a smile rests easy on her face. No longer reeling from lost loves, she is satisfied with how her life turned out. Jaime's first love would always be there, cemented in her heart. There would never be anyone else to take his place. She tended to the new generation of horses that were born to their nurturing mares. She felt motherly watching the animals care for their young. It was her wish to do the same for own daughter. Jaime will go on to live a full life.

A mother's love is always there for her children. For Jaime Sanderson, love grew after Cara came into her life. She sits in her living room, with her husband near her and closes her eyes. She relives those memories of connecting with her family and all of the times they spent together. There is forgiveness and a heartfelt feeling of knowing that new memories will grow with each generation. Derek puts his hand on hers happy to see her content. His hard work has finally paid off. He has the loving and involved family he longed for.

For Cara and T.J., there is nothing they won't do to get through many of the changes young married couples go through in their life together. Cara observed how her blindness changed her perception of what her life would be like. She learned when to rely on others, especially the man who never judged her or her past. Cara used her sense of touch to make her smile. Touching the flowers, trees, horses, and the faces of new people she met kept life intriguing.

In a few years Cara will become the mother of two daughters, Daisy and Hanna. Thew will grow up just like her, falling in love with riding and disliking lessons. T.J. will give his daughters what they need; the closeness of two parents who know how to give true love. Cara knows that generations down the line will remember her and Jaime and their unique story of love lost and found.

"Thank you, Jocelyn," Patrick says.

"For what?"

"For being alive, for being here. After I lost my grandfather, you were there to make me feel alive again.

Thank you for being my wife. Thank you for being my family."

Jocelyn wraps her arms around Patrick as she thinks of her family living across the field and how they were able to heal with love. She notices Cara standing next her horse stroking his mane. The setting sunlight is illuminating her body. She glows softly like a beautiful painting. No one would suspect her sightless.

Cara is a found and complete woman. She knows who she is, a woman who is gifted no matter what she went through to find her family.

T.J. plans to take his family to Lindley Park and carve their names on their tree. He will tell his girls the story about how he met their mother and what the tree means to them. There will be a special spot where their names will live inside a carved heart. Their daughters will climb and sit in the same branches as their parents did years ago. They will put their mark next to theirs. Cara will sit below and cherish the sound of their laughter and voices as they play. Many years will go by and as long as the tree at Lindley Park lives, those names will live on and will be visible to all. There is a story behind their carvings. Cara and T.J.'s story.

For Jaime Sanderson

Annette Stephenson

The Tree at Lindley Park

www.ingramcontent.com/pod-product-compliance
Lightning Source LLC
Chambersburg PA
CBHW060926120626
46557CB00003B/887